"The sign on the road to Derbyville should read 'Welcome to the Apocalypse of the Innocents.' Matthew Derby's zanily inventive fictional world will disarm you with its bleak humor, its dire and giddy sentences, its irrepressible sense of wonder, its urgent narrative force. Prepare to laugh, to be uplifted, to be a tiny bit ruined." —HEIDI JULAVITS, author of *The Mineral Palace*

"I can't believe I'm writing this sentence, but Derby's book is a bold step forward in science fiction. Imagine *The Matrix,* but funny, or a neurotic *Metropolis,* and you might get some sense of what this weird, beautifully written book, made by someone who has watched far too much television, does to your brain."
—NEAL POLLACK, author of
The Neal Pollack Anthology of American Literature

"Matthew Derby stages a wagon circle around everything dull and earthbound in American fiction. His stories arrive in an almost fantastical mode, shimmering with broken robots and strange machines, but their sense of doom, hilarity, and overwhelming grief comes directly from the real world. A vital and astonishing writer."
—BEN MARCUS, author of *The Age of Wire and String* and *Notable American Women*

"These stories are hilarious, the dialogue is pitch-perfect, as if you're listening in on the last minutes of doomed men in a bunker who have no idea they're doomed. These are about the only sentences I would say actually have acoustics. The stories took me out of this world and into a more interesting one. Derby's characters are helpless, angry, and very seductive, and his decrepit, futuristic world is both wonderful and terrible and entirely too credible."
—RJ CURTIS

Super Flat Times

Stories

Matthew Derby

Little, Brown and Company

Boston New York London

Grateful acknowledgment is made to the following publications in which some of these stories were first published: "Instructions," *5 Trope;* "Home Recordings," *3rd bed;* "Joy of Eating," *Conjunctions;* "The Father Helmet," *Fence;* "The Boyish Mulatto," *American Journal of Print;* "Meat Tower," *Elimae;* "Behavior Pilot," *Failbetter;* "Sky Harvest," *Pindeldyboz*

Library of Congress Cataloging-in-Publication Data
Derby, Matthew.
    Super flat times : stories / Matthew Derby.
       p. cm.
    ISBN 0-316-73857-3
       1. Technology and civilization — Fiction.   2. Science fiction,
American.   I. Title.
    PS3604.E73 S87 2003
    813'.6 — dc21   2002034131

10   9   8   7   6   5   4   3   2   1

Q–FF

Book designed by Jonathan D. Lippincott

Printed in the United States of America

For Mary-Kim and Zooey

Contents

Is history ever just "past," really over? Recognizing the specific social circumstances, the ideological development and material differences hardly breaks the thread — just splits it, like a net cast wide.

— Mimi Nguyen

Super Flat Times

F irst they took men. Heavy ones — men that might sink to the bottom. In secret they stormed the towns, the suburbs, the complexes. They bound the men's hands behind their backs and marched them out to the foothills or into ravines, anywhere low enough so that no one would see. They lined them up along the edge of the deep concrete pools they'd built, whispered brief slogans into the men's ears, and then shoved them, face first, into the quickening substance. When the heavy ones were all accounted for, they took men who struggled, men who hid, men with sharp tongues, men with hair on their backs, men named Kevin. The men who did not resist, the men who were willing to die, were sent off to fight wars instead. When men grew scarce, they took children, and when the children thinned out they tossed women into the gritty, viscous pits. Then they moved on to the next region. We never knew what the executioners were after, only that each time they were through, there were fewer of us for the killing.

The concrete pools have since been converted to parks, and those of us who have been allowed to remember (or, *Those of Us*

Who Have Been Allowed to Remember) feel that this was the right thing to do. But it has become clear that these public gathering spaces are not enough, that some more substantial document of this era is necessary. These were the Super Flat Times, after all — years that did not seem to pass so much as inflate crazily to the bursting point, break, and collapse, withered and damp, only to be replaced by another weepy, indistinguishable abrasion. That we survived at all is a monument in itself, but we will soon pass, and the parks, too, will gradually lose their meaning, as each successive generation of children wears the concrete structures down to pillowy stumps with their play. There will be those who will claim that the executions did not happen, that they could not possibly have happened, and every year the temptation to give yourself over to this impression will grow. That is why we have decided to produce this document, a living record of the past, so that you who have been spared the memory of what you went through, what you narrowly survived, can understand. We at the Hall of Those Who Have Been Allowed to Remember have decided that it must be a document for families, a book to be placed on a wooden lectern and read aloud at gatherings. An article through which the unbearable truth of these years might be preserved.

We decided right away that an account of our own remembrance would prove so extraordinarily spotty that it would only drive this period further into obscurity. It is true that we were allowed to keep our memories because of the great care with which we'd mentally catalogued what we saw during the Super Flat Times, but nobody in our group felt capable of putting it into words. In the first years after the Great Severance, we could barely write down a Daily Personal Emotion Statement without having to douse our heads in the static bucket to stop them from quivering, much less attempt to convey a string of memories so painful that wincing had become our default facial expression. The volume, we decided, should give those who did not survive the one last chance to air their grievances that never came to them in life. By drilling down into the concrete pools, we were able to extract their last breaths, piercing with a sharp metal straw the tiny crescent-shaped sac of air forced out of their lungs as they collapsed under the weight of the rapidly solidifying medium. This air, once isolated in a glass cabinet at the Hall of Memory and massaged by a professional translator, can sometimes reveal the Missing Person's final thoughts. Those of us who have been allowed to remember refer to the resultant documents, the clearest of which you are about to read, as prayers.

I should warn you — not all of the prayers in this volume render with the precision that, perhaps, was felt by their original authors. Please keep in mind that the Missing Persons had no way of knowing at the time that their execution would be recorded by our organization years later. The great majority of relevant data is occluded by fits of shouting, flailing, or violent outbursts such as "Please help me die," "I can't feel my shoulders," or "Someone I hate is on top of me." (I have excised these intrusive bits only wherever their presence would otherwise hamper the flow of the prayer.) Other factors have conspired against an accurate representation as well — the persistent nausea we suffered while massaging the texts in the deep underground bunkers of the Hall (as you know, the air must be churned sometimes for hours in order to yield the fragile memory pockets), for example, and the single yellow elimination bucket we were allowed to carry down, a receptacle that brimmed always at day's end with meaty, clotted waste. At times, the nausea was so intense that parts of us broke off while we vomited. Hence, my missing hand. None of this made our job any easier.

The first years, 5 to 50, are greatly underrepresented, primarily because of the incredibly poor condition of the prayers. The government's attempts to advertise on the atmosphere through the use of colored gas, or Fud, and the ensuing accretion of hard chunks of air — what we now call Clouds — have so polluted and obfuscated the prayers that many of the remaining texts contain just a few recognizable words or gestures, readable only with the most sensitive horned instruments. Air samples taken from the North and Northwestern Properties, where the Meat Initiative was enforced starting in Year 7, are also difficult to manage, given that a sustained all-meat diet tends to deaden the lungs. Still other prayers contain only the fragile ululations that accompanied the words, and there is little that can be done to preserve them. One can still *feel* these works, but their translation into English III is impossible. This is regrettable, but it is hoped that what is left might be of some help in illustrating the period.

The reader will note a great many more prayers devoted to Year 51, proportionally, than to the years before or after. My reasons are embarrassingly personal. By Year 51, the government's Population Redistribution and Elimination Program had failed in its efforts to contain and manage regional population and to maintain significant racial attributes solely through its weekly instructional radio hour. Over 70 percent of the world's population was of mixed or untraceable racial heritage, and the population had increased 15 percent above acceptable loss, mostly because of illegal or unmonitored childbirth. The Royal Child Harvest was enforced in order to build an emergency egg repository and to formalize the population-control enterprise. Although my Culture Visa enabled me to work in the administrative offices of The Factories instead of on the workshop floor (I sorted fabric swatches and sounded the meeting gong), I was required nonetheless to surrender two eggs a year (and so, thankfully, only two eggs) to the Ministry of Child Harvesting. Women I interviewed in preparation for this project claimed I was lucky — lifting their tunics to reveal the twin flesh flaps, sealed shut with red plastic buttons, that covered their uterine holes, they spoke of the humiliating abdominal specula, the steel calipers, the bitter aftertaste of the generative pills that, when processed by the body, yielded up to nine thousand eggs a month, grapefruit-sized clusters that often broke the carrier's hips, so that they walked forever afterward like angry, three-wheeled vegetable carts. But for me these words are of little comfort. These women, the donors, will always be able to take comfort in the sheer number of eggs they produced — their children are bound to be somewhere, at least one in every city. I yielded only two. Two untraceable eggs, lost in the world. Until the eggs were taken from me the whole proposition of childbirth bored me. The idea that I could somehow replicate myself in miniature seemed a reckless waste of time, but I have carried them to term in my mind so often now that I could sculpt their bulging, sloppy faces from behind a heavy blindfold. How close I have become to them, how frequently I have knelt beside their twin cribs, watching them go slack in the night, overcome with exhaustion. Tape a pencil to my atrophied wrist and I could render an intricate cardiograph for each rasping heart. But what really happened to them? Where are they now? In whose house have they been working themselves up, shakily, toward adulthood? Who else do they dare call mother, father, sister? I have often found myself loitering outside the memorial parks, clutching the wire fencing with one scaly, whitened hand, searching for some recognizable trait. Irrational as it seems, I am sure I could pick them, sight unseen, out of a crowd. It could be that my whole purpose in excavating these prayers has had to do with the improbable dream that I might find my children somewhere deep in the concrete, that their final thoughts might make a brief appearance in my palm. So far, nothing has surfaced.

The third era documented here — the period after the failure of the Royal Child Harvest and before the Great Severance, the Race Census — is illegal for me to reflect upon. I will say only that those of us who lived, lived through *it*. I had a husband during this period who was only part Korean. He didn't go missing until three years into our relationship, right at the end, but there were near misses all the time. Once, on a crowded subway, he switched places with a meat farmer so that the farmer, who had a tired, dry face, could sit. At the next stop, the lights went out briefly, and when they came back on, the farmer was gone. Another time we were on a tiny sailboat in the bay. It was dark out — we'd temporarily stolen the boat from the amusement park. I was drowsy from too much wine. I put my hand in the water and immediately felt something move, something with the texture of rough, soaked cloth. There was a body swimming there, possibly two. I threw myself on my husband, who was asleep. "Leave us alone," I shouted, but there was no answer, only the water lapping against the crude hull of the boat.

Some maintain that the disappearances, the mass executions, were a gift for the victims; at least they did not have to suffer the indignity of whatever came next. I could not possibly agree more. I saw secret executions from my office window, hundreds of them. I was told not to look, to keep my head down as I riffled through the fabric swatch bricks, but sometimes out of the corner of my eye I could see a single arm flailing on the surface of the thick gray pool, a fleeting, primitive white flag. I'd look away, and when I looked back all that was left was a finger. One time it was a woman's head. I swear she was looking right at me, staring at me evenly as she sank. I remember thinking only how beautiful she looked, and how utterly calm. I kept thinking about the woman for months afterward. Whenever I thought of her I became irrationally angry. At first, I thought that the anger came from indignation, but eventually, as the thought of sinking into the damp substrate became more tempting, I came to understand it as a kind of jealousy.

And what will you have come away with after the last translated prayer has been read? You who have been fortunate enough to have had the whole history of the Super Flat Times swept from your head by the memory surgeons, so that all you remember is sitting up in the expansive Recovery Hall on Liberation Day with a bandage on your forehead and a sick taste in your mouth, how will you digest this volume? I hope that, above all things, you have not opened this book in order to learn. Because it is not what has been learned in these years that makes those of us who have been allowed to remember crumple with deep nausea every time we look back, but what has *not* been learned, the secret language we have carried in our bodies throughout these ordeals, in spite of them, the navigational matter coiled tightly in our hearts like the springs in a clock-work toy, gestures we sprung on one another in dense, over-crowded basement camps, in regenerative supermarket aisles, in the public showers, fussily breathing whole histories into the ear of whoever should be unluckily close. What we have learned will expire, but these things we have not learned will survive us. We pass these things along despite ourselves, and are nothing more or less than what we do with the rest of our time. Mean-while, we are swelling with the unthought thoughts, hurling them out into the world like dead skin, temporary hosts for the larger, terminal memory.

Seoul II,
17 Tworuary, 67
Mi Jin Ahn-Strauss

Years 5—50

My stepfather was among the first to go. Days after he disappeared, we found his wig on the front porch. Whoever had taken him away had brought the wig back. There were things about him that weren't even worth throwing away. My mother lifted the wig gently, as if it were a hurt animal, and brought it inside. For years no one spoke of his disappearance, and the wig remained on a table in the front hall. Then one day the wig was gone, and my brother found a small headstone in the garden, near a patch of freshly turned soil. He brought me back to show me the grave, and when he pointed at the tiny, misshapen stone he said only, "Get used to this," before heading out to the barn where he made meatloaf for the soldiers.

We hardly noticed the first Food Ban. There was a piece on the news about a cabbage virus, and then the cabbage stand was gone from the market. We were secretly relieved about the cabbage — no need to think up new ways to fix that particular item. It went this way with the other foods, until only meat was safe. Some people on our street held a small protest at the market, but then they were gone as well. We knew that something was wrong, that something essential was being hoisted from our grasp, but at the same time, meat was the one food we really liked to eat. An all-meat diet was something we'd been unconsciously looking forward to, like the cooling storm that breaks a heat wave.

Meanwhile, there was a boy in our school who had been held back a year because he was slow. When the new Recruitment Initiative went into effect, he found he was too old to get a good job. He kept asking his parents to make him younger. Every time they told him no. "That is not the direction you were meant to grow," they said, but he found a way to grow down anyway. He found a way to shed his age by eating pebbles and soaking himself in heavy water. One day he saw the hair on his leg start to retreat. "Now we're getting somewhere," he thought.

He got a job right away, one of the best available. In a month he was second-in-command at Corporation Two. He bought a high-speed boat, a rare poisonous snake, two rocket launchers, and a magnificent house for his parents. Every night he ate dinner with them at a long wooden table, punctuating the deep silence only to ask mockingly if they would let him grow younger. They only bowed their heads, shamefully forking around massive helpings of beef on gilded plates.

We are dragging it by hand now. The engine gave out days ago in a ravine two kilometers south of the parallel. We managed to haul the weapon out of the deep, fecal muck with two stolen mules, which were of no use to us once we ran out of the dried ice cream, the only thing that would get them moving. We killed the mules and ate them, and now we are dragging the Sound Gun by hand, using the last of the rope and medical gauze. No one is happy about this, not even Shaving Gel, whom we call Shaving Gel because he always smells like shaving gel, although we should call him Bulk or Keg or Mountain because he is big. I speculated that he, out of any of them, would champion the cause, shouldering the weapon from behind, barking fiercely at the enlisted men. Instead, he just looked at me evenly from the other side of the campfire, chewing deliberately at his mule as I debriefed the group.

Nobody knows what we are doing here. We are not entirely sure that the war is still happening. Since the mules ate the communications array we have had only the color of the sky to guide us. Evenings, it will burst suddenly into a thin purple halo of dense mist. These rings, we believe, must be the fragrant shards of battles occurring elsewhere in secret. So we continue to plow through the jungle, convinced that, any day now, a dark, backlit man in a business suit will descend from the sky in a clear pod and usher us home.

It was fun to drive around in the Sound Gun until it stopped working. Now the people who are fighting us, and who we are pretty sure are still the enemy, are much more dangerous and harder to kill. They come rushing up at us in the night, tossing sticks and VCRs.

My men go on about the size of the Sound Gun. Everything else is smaller now than in previous wars, but the Sound Gun is unimaginably bigger. "Bigger than what?" I ask Danson in a fit, having overheard this complaint for the last time.

"It's just bigger than it should be, sir," says Danson, a slight, walleyed Presbyterian who carries his recently deceased mother's dialysis machine with him at all times in a bowling ball bag, just in case or as a memento — no one knows for sure. "It should be, like, calculator-size. The size of a handheld — help me someone — think of something handheld . . ."

"A gun," says Memorex.

"Yes, exactly. All we ask is that the Sound Gun be the actual size of a gun? Instead of, like, a whole building?"

"Write it down in your Wish Journal, Private," I tell him. Everyone has a Wish Journal. When we're sad or upset or feeling violent we write in the Wish Journal. "I wish I could wrap my feelings in burlap and throw them into the ocean," we might write, or "I wish the act of sleep actually came with a blanket" or "I wish just one of my fellow soldiers was even remotely as attractive as the ones in the advertisements on the cloud screens, the ones climbing wooden structures with their shirts off or getting pummeled with a long, padded brick."

The Sound Gun has four settings. The first one is Make Scared. Make Scared makes a big loud noise that makes people scared. It is louder and scarier than the noise a bomb makes as it explodes, because the people we're fighting have not been scared by that sound for three wars. The sound that Make Scared makes is like a herd of elk tumbling into a cauldron of hot, resonant dung or, at night, the frail puff of air conjured up by a dying child. Make Scared worked for a while, but then the enemy started putting soaked wheat pods in their ears, so we had to move on to Hurt.

Hurt feels like getting hit hard by a rubber blanket. Not that I'd know — this is what the instructions tell us: "Stay out of the path of the Sound Gun when using Hurt mode; otherwise, you may be struck by the slug with the force of a large rubber blanket." Hurt worked for a longer time than Make Scared, because nobody liked having these rubber blankets constantly hurled at her. But the enemy developed a flared aluminum instrument, worn on the hips, that sprayed a hard yellow foam so that they could build tall, ad hoc baffles while advancing on us. We were left with no alternative: we had to switch to Very Hurt.

All the officers have been given a captured enemy soldier as a pet. I'm sickened by this practice, but own one myself and have to admit I have grown considerably dependent on the little man. In an attempt to distance myself from some of the more undesirable aspects of the relationship, I've named him Constantine. It's a dignified name, I think — much more dignified than Bastard Face, Shovel, or Milk of Magnesia, names that have been bestowed upon others in our midst. He has not, as of yet, become comfortable with it. Otherwise, he plays the role of slave with outrageous conviction, leaning into his servitude with an enthusiasm that mars my ability to sympathize with his plight. I want him to be belligerent or distant — anything but eager. Each morning by the time I wake up he's already gone off looking for kindling or is turning the spit on which a tube of meat product sizzles over a roaring fire. It is the worst, most diabolical revenge, and he knows it.

Very Hurt mode kept the enemy at bay for a good while. During that time, though, we heard from headquarters less and less. We started getting stark, austere communiqués like "Swell forest," "Stab the fabric cone," and "Fork" — dense, barely pronounceable phrases, indicating a new plateau of military strategy no one in our ranks could unpack. Our objective here, once clear and urgent, had faded into obscurity. The mission had become so secret that it had disappeared altogether. This made us angry, and tired. No one wanted to deal with all of the Very Hurt soldiers lying around, as they had to be dragged out of the path of the Sound Gun before we could move it. With no one to instruct us otherwise, we cranked up the gun from Very Hurt to Make Dead. Make Dead ruptures the enemy's bowels as the blast hurls them twenty feet or more into the air.

In Make Dead mode the frequency is so low that you can no longer hear the gun as it fires — only the sound the enemy soldiers make as they sail through the air, limbs flapping like damp cloth.

I do not miss home, but not for the usual reasons. I like home, generally, but I do not like home the way that I left it — with a large wild bobcat living there. I came home one night and found Gruver on all fours, peering under the couch, where the bobcat was hiding. As the bobcat was a very large animal, this was not the best place to hide. The couch was balanced on its back, see-sawing back and forth while Gruver offered up warm, encouraging aphorisms.

"I do not want to hear it," he said when I asked what was under the couch. I did not then know that what was under the couch was, in actuality, a bobcat. A bobcat, at that time, was one of the very last things I was thinking of.

"I found this beautiful animal in the garbage can, and it is now mine," Gruver called out from the floor.

"Clearly," I said.

"I will not hear any arguments against my case."

I saw that Gruver's left arm was bandaged with a shredded, bloodied T-shirt. "It's nothing," he said preemptively, cupping the wounded elbow with his free hand.

I went upstairs and ate a Starburst on the bed.

"Why don't you come down here," Gruver shouted from the bottom of the stairs. "Why don't you come down and put your hand on this animal's flanks? Feel the strength just lying there, dormant."

"It's sulking," I called out. "It is bringing down the whole house with that attitude."

"He's been abandoned. I believe that this animal has got a definite right to sulk?"

I had been with Gruver for seven years. Suddenly, it did not seem like such a good idea.

"Constantine," I call out from my tent. He sits cross-legged by the fire, facing away from me, worrying the coals with a slender branch. His shadow flickers wildly on the green nylon wall of the tent, the shape of his body crassly drawing attention to itself, showboating there behind him on the makeshift scrim, taunting me with the suggestion that, given half the chance, it might swallow me whole, enveloping the tent itself, the camp, everything we have brought along. "Constantine, bring me my flask." He does not move. He wants me to call him by his given name, which is Idrissa. He sits and waits.

On my way to the latrine I see Memorex sitting on a felled tree, writing in his Wish Journal.

"Well, hard at work, I see," I say, trying to amount to something in his mind.

"I'm just writing," he says.

I kneel at his side, laying a hand on his thigh, giving it a brief, reassuring squeeze. It is not an advance; I'd rather dip my face into a bucket of glass shards than sidle up to Memorex's whitened, porous midriff, but it's taken as such, and I get a frightened grimace.

I pull my hand away. "Sometimes the hurt goes away when we talk, too."

Memorex rests his pen in the spine. "I wish we weren't killing people."

The phrase "killing people" jars me — in my mind it isn't so much killing people that we are engaged in as pushing them out of the way, except that they stay there, wherever they topple, forever. "Well, Memorex, you know that's not a Wish Journal wish. That's not a feeling. You can't, you know, put that anywhere."

"I feel something about it, though. To see all those people go flying up in the air, all, like, ruptured? I feel something when that happens. It's, like, really a feeling, like getting hit in the face with a basketball again and again —"

"Like the time at base camp —"

"Yes. Just like. What is that feeling?"

"I don't know, Memorex. But it doesn't sound like the kind of feeling that winners feel. Is it? Is that the way you think people who win feel? Do you think that General Custer, as he stood atop the mound of enemy corpses, felt the way that you're feeling?"

He rubs the side of his face where scabs from a constellation of wicked-huge spider bites pill and drift. "No, that's definitely not what winners feel."

"Well, you've answered your own question there, Memorex, haven't you?"

"Yeah?"

"Yes. The answer is, don't feel feelings that aren't winning feelings. Make sense?"

Memorex nods and continues his journal entry. I run to the

latrine, buckling, suddenly, with waste. I fill to the brim nearly five Mason jars.

The enemy is getting smarter. They start digging big holes, which they cover up with leafy tree branches. They dig the holes so well and disguise them so carefully that, eventually, we fall into one. I hit the ground shoulder first, half of me sucked instantly into a pool of mud. Conservarte falls on top of me, his left knee coming down directly on my solar plexus. "Sorry, sir," he whispers, splashing frantically in the thick puddle. I grip his upper arm to shush him, pointing up toward the mouth of the giant hole. Everything goes dark and quiet as the Sound Gun teeters at the edge. Danson and his slave, who are tethered to the machine with the medical gauze, dangle about four meters from the ground, flailing their limbs erratically. Slowly, with groaning indecision, the Sound Gun begins to tip forward, and then, with unimaginable speed, casting out a heavy sheet of debris, it falls, landing on top of the both of them.

When the cloud dissipates, all we can see of them are their legs, sticking out from the treads like beefy shards of driftwood. Constantine rushes over to help Danson's slave, who used to be his wife, but the upper half of her has been completely squashed. He pulls on one of the legs for a while, whimpering, desperately imploring us to join in. We all look down or away, or up at the mouth of the hole, anything to avoid his plaintive stare.

If dragging the Sound Gun out of the ravine with four sturdy, if belligerent, mules was difficult, dragging it out of a surprisingly deep, narrow hole with no mules is all but impossible, but in the afternoon Memorex gets the idea that we could blast a path out of the ground. We have never tried shooting at the ground before, but given what usually happens when we

shoot the Sound Gun, what with the leveling of trees and barri-
cades, the hoisting aloft of enemy soldiers, the hurling of bodies, high and far, and so forth, moving earth seems eminently
feasible. We all grab our percussion suits and take off into the
brush while Conservarte warms up the generator.

"Okay," he calls out when everyone is far enough away.
"Christ if I'm not going to do this." He grunts for a while,
fiercely turning switches.

We pull the rip cords on the inflatable suits, biting down on the
hard plastic mouthpieces. Air rushes into the stiff fabric, puffing us
up like ripe berries. There is a moment of absolute silence, and
then a faint crackling sound before a fierce shock wave knocks us
back on our asses. Snakes and other creatures start falling out of the
trees. One falls on my face and I jump up, flailing wildly. We are
safe because we are in the percussion suits. But still.

Momentarily, the earth settles. The creatures of the forest,
those that survived, have been shocked into silence. By the tree
line an enormous brown creature lies on its side, twitching. We
deflate our suits and make our way back to the hole. Conservarte
is peering out over the wide, dual barrel of the Sound Gun. The
hole is measurably bigger. We walk its perimeter to make sure.

"Did you put it up all the way?" I ask, but, since I forgot to
remove my mouthpiece, what it sounds like is "Duh duh duh
duh duh duh duh duh?"

"She's cranked, sir."

"Let's give it another shot."

It is dark out. The hole is bigger, I tell them. Look. They only
look down into their plates of gruel, willing it into anything but
the gray assemblage steaming away before them. We can hear

the enemy cackling in the distance. I climb into the cockpit and
fire off a round into the trees, snapping the trunks in half. The
cackling stops.

After dinner, gathered as we are around a pathetic campfire
made from Danson's boots, Memorex carefully draws a small
photograph from his breast pocket, cupping it gently in his
palm. Shaving Gel and Orange Face sheepishly follow suit. It is
against the rules for the men to carry photographs, but who am
I to enforce rules? After ordering Conservarte to crank the settings of the Sound Gun from Very Hurt to Make Dead, a con-
figuration that hadn't ever really been tested, let alone approved?
After taking the men deeper and deeper into the unmapped
wilderness, following a set of military objectives I'd constructed
by vague speculation? Who am I to snatch the photographs the
men have carried around with them at great risk, images of
their dumb, savage loved ones, and toss them into the dwindling
campfire?

I snatch the photographs the men have carried around with
them at great risk and toss them into the dwindling campfire.

Gruver whispered something from across the room. It was my
last night in New Jersey, one that I had willfully hacked away at
on the Boardwalk, stuffing myself with sticky buns while standing in line for brightly lit amusement rides that, if successful,
would bring the heavy pastry back up. I shouted and growled at
anyone who dared occupy the vacant passenger seat of my
bumper car — I arched my back like a banshee, if that is indeed

what banshees do, and hissed at them, spraying their faces with murky brown mist. I wanted to ward off all human contact, to create the narrowest possible aperture in the world through which to jettison myself.

Things had not been going so well between the bobcat and me, so for the past week or so I'd been sleeping in the closet, curled up like a fetal chick in the corner. The two of them slept in the big yellow bed, the cat's disturbing, furry head nestled in the crook of Gruver's arm. Every night I watched them through the crack in the closet door until I fell unconscious, lulled to sleep by the animal's heavy breathing. On the last night, though, I left the closet door open. Should the cat climb onto my back and bounce repeatedly, as if I were an unsteady outcropping of rock, then so be it. There were more undignified ways to go out than to be crushed by a wild animal.

The cat, though, did not climb onto my back. Instead, I woke in a dyspeptic haze to Gruver's thick, malleable face staring at me from across the room, suspended, it seemed, from the doorframe. He whispered something, this head floating at the entrance to what had been our room. I could not hear him, though; what came out of his mouth sounded like "gretl balls."

"Come again?" I said, shooting up from the tangled sheets piled up on the closet floor, but it sounded more like a plea than a question, and before I had fully understood what was happening he was gone — the soft head withdrawn into the hallway and out the door.

The Sound Gun was made so that we could fight friendlier wars. The Wish Journals are so that we can fight with clean consciences. The no-pictures rule is so that we forget what we're missing. The slaves we made up. Also the deaths. And our reason for being here. That part was made up when the mules ate part of the communications array.

Eating the mules, we made up.

We have started digging a path with shovels fashioned from hollowed-out tree trunks. At the rate we're currently proceeding, we'll be finished by Saturday. The Sound Gun may not be working, though. It's settled into the hole at an angle, engine and auxiliary generators submerged in a clammy pool of mud. Whenever we turn the key it only shudders briefly, offering up a thin plume of green smoke, and then dies, leaving a deafening silence in its wake. Conservarte is inside the cockpit, working with an oversize wrench in an attempt to breathe some life into the machine.

"God, I'm starting to think of my house," Memorex blurts out suddenly, collapsing to his knees. "I'm thinking of my house with everything inside of it. I'm thinking of a piece of floor inside my house that has junk all over it and if someone cleans up the junk without me there I won't ever be able to find it again and put it together because it's not really junk it's my diabetes kit —"

"Hey, hey," I call over to him, "no need to panic, there. Let's all take out our Wish Journals, men, and start writing away Memorex's bad feelings. Get out your Wish Journals —"

"No," says Memorex, "no, I *want* to feel this way. I want to.

Don't anybody put my feelings in a canvas bag." The rest of the men look up from their freshly opened journals, pens carefully poised over the ruled sheets. Memorex slides down the mud ramp on his knees, coming to rest underneath one of the enormous armored treads of the Sound Gun, where he slumps like an old, head-beaten pillow.

"Memorex," I say, crawling backward down the steep trail that he has just plowed with his body. "What's this bit of silliness? Come now, your house is not important anymore. Your car, your tile sample collection, your whole life just pales in comparison to what you're doing here. We're fighting a war here, Memorex."

"War? This is a war?"

"Yes, Memorex, of course."

"What is the war about?" he asks from under the tread. All we can see are his legs. Constantine turns away. "I can't remember what the war is about, so maybe you can just, like, tell me?"

"Memorex. It's not really our place to ask, is it? I mean, you wanted to disappear, correct? You wanted never to have happened, am I right? That is the reason you and the rest of us are here, correct? We are men in retreat, all of us. We are hiding from the rest of our lives. The terms have always been fairly well defined. Otherwise, they never would have signed you up. Now come on, Memorex, let's crawl our way out of the mud, shall we?"

The legs don't move. "I'm going to lie here until I get crushed."

Constantine turns back toward Memorex's legs, bending at the waist in prayer.

"What's that he's saying?" I ask Shaving Gel, who points the translation gun at Constantine's head.

"Says he's not leaving, either. He wants to die, too, so that he can be with his wife."

Memorex starts chanting along phonetically with Constantine. Constantine crawls in next to Memorex, so all that we can see are their legs, four sets now, poking out from underneath the tread.

We are there for a long time, watching the two of them shudder and yelp like Pentecostals under the Sound Gun. It is not clear what we should do at this point.

"Sir," Shaving Gel asks, saluting halfheartedly as he approaches.

"Yes, Shaving Gel."

"With all due permission, sir, can we break from this, like, vigil-type thing?"

"Absolutely not."

"Sir, how come?"

"Because these two are being ridiculous, and we must show them that we, too, can be ridiculous. We must suffocate them with our will."

"Oh," Shaving Gel says, looking down at his feet. "Can I at least have a sandwich?"

I imagine the look I give Shaving Gel to be wild with disbelief. "Where did you get a sandwich from?"

"Well, sir, it's a dirt sandwich."

"A dirt sandwich."

"Yes, sir."

I take a survey of the other men. They are all watching, shovels pitched defiantly into the mud. Their eyes are black and distant, the opposite of stars. "Shaving Gel," I say, grasping his shoulder paternally, "by all means, go have yourself a dirt sandwich." He lopes off happily into the brush, disappearing behind a spray of wiry vines. The rest of the men do not move.

In the morning I am the only one left. Shaving Gel has not returned. I can see by the muddy prints left on the crispy shale that the Numismatist has scaled the high cliff wall to the east sometime during the night, last of the mule meat and ice tubes strapped to his back. Orange Face has left a small shrine fashioned from twigs and diaphanous gauze, the significance of which is not entirely lost on me. Half Brick and his two slaves are simply gone without a trace — they have even taken the body floss and the elimination hood.

Actually, I should not say that I am the only one left. Memorex and Constantine remain under the Sound Gun, keening like abandoned kittens. As far as anyone that matters is concerned, however, I am the only one left, where "anyone that matters" equals the part of me that does not go off like the others, abandoning the Sound Gun and the mission. Missions are important, I tell myself. They are important, and they are to be carried out. Every bit as important as a person.

I am resting on the gnarled trunk of a felled tree, and it has just occurred to me how comfortable an object it is, how well it accepts my intrusive ass, utterly without condescension, without the attendant grief brought on by contemporary furniture. How quiet a thing the world is without all these crude, puffy bodies flailing away at it. I long for a cigarette, and for the first time since I have been here, I long, also, for Gruver, towering over me, shaking me from my sleep for an early walk. I long for his fierce, stubbled head; his long, recriminatory stares; and the way that he would grasp my jaw when we coupled, his filthy fingers in my mouth, clamping my tongue flat, as though he could, by holding down my face, perform a hostile takeover of the burdensome life I'd absently flung at him, neutralizing, at last, the dull tyranny of language.

Let them pray, is what I am thinking here at the bottom of the enemy hole. Let them pray for atonement, and may the purest heart rise up, out of this flat land and back to the first place that seemed a good idea to stay away from.

I was, above all other things, a woman with a situation. A hard, looming truth had been rubbed into me like a curative ointment, the kind that leaves its faint, crusted mark for good. To get to the point: I weathered a foreshortened family, I endured what were to become the battered last days of a life I was sure I'd barely live to regret.

All of us were in the future, where we belonged. It actually *was* the future — a period of time that so embodied what we thought the future would be like that the government had to replace the term with a new one, *fufier*, in order to designate the grim, impending series of events that had not yet occurred. Those were the years of corporate oligarchy, of videophonic telephones, meal tablets, and robot hearts. Years of silver foil and mass, private flight. We were observed, things were expected of us, a green pill was created to help us remember when to take a certain blue pill. We did all the important things and let the old and the sick work in The Factories. This was a time of sadly predictable oppression and digital surveillance. What was most vital about our lives was recorded and stored on a government database, which was looked upon with such utter detachment that we often forgot it was there. We were, above all, children, barely fit for the sort of lives we led.

When we wanted meat, what we got was meat. When we wanted a morning constitutional, however, what we got was also meat. Meat, it appeared, was all there was left — great, heaping stacks of it, stored in icy towers at the center of the city, tended to by large men in white masks and rubber boots who wielded pitchforks and prods. We learned to shape the meat, to flavor it in such a way that we might not forget what it was like to taste an apple, say — to bite through the ruddy skin, which gave way to the sweet, tender center. We could achieve this effect with spiced, cured ham, stuffed into a tough intestinal sack. Chocolate was hard to eat for those of us who could remember the real thing. Children, though, loved to chew upon the hard, brittle cubes of browned beef that came wrapped delicately in gold foil. Cheese was meat. Juice was meat. Porksicles. Beefsicles. Baconsicles. This was the fulcrum from which our lives precariously swung.

Chocolate milk was still milk, but the chocolate was made from hard, shaved splinters of seasoned loin. It had a sour, syrupy aftertaste — those of us who remembered called it simply "chilk" in an effort to preserve the dignity of the earlier, more substantial drink. But the children took in chilk whenever it was offered — how greedy they seemed, always clamoring like blind puppies to take the nozzle to their trembling, puckered lips.

The meat made us look different. We got fat for a while — years, actually — but then the fat left us, so that what we were left with were baggy flaps of limp, oily skin, whole bolts of extra body. We gathered this loose flesh in long, flat clips at our shoulders, so that the worst among us appeared to have wings.

The disappearance of a sustainable agriculture was a regrettable side effect of the Ministry of Air and Justice's efforts, in the years of Fud, to color the air, to advertise the act of breathing with pale, pastel tints that bloomed upon exhalation. The air dispersed by the Fud Bellows did not color the air as promised but ascended, instead, into the pathetic, overwrought stratosphere, gathering there in hard, dark, permanent clouds. Few of us, though, were sufficiently interested in what went on above us to bother complaining — it seemed foolish to continue with the charade that the sky was anything more than wasted space, a vast area that could be put to much better use.

Meanwhile, there was a man to whom I'd found myself married, and a child whom we'd drawn up between us not long afterward, like a bucket from a deep well. The three of us heaved away in a choked-up studio apartment on the humid side of the city, the side whereat the clouds hung so low as to scrape glacially past our windows, carving dull swaths across the panes, so that what light we did get was diffuse, splotchy. The clouds frightened the child, Philip; when they passed he'd crawl inside the big panda suit and huddle in the doorframe. The panda suit, we'd taught him — it was soft and warm, like a blanket, something to make him feel safe — but the doorframe seemed particularly anachronistic; something he'd picked up, impossibly, from an old Civil Defense manual. We were disturbed by this behavior and made every effort not to look at the child as he huddled there, shivering in the fur suit, while the passing clouds gently rocked the building.

My husband was a face attendant, unemployed. When he

was working, his job was to stand next to his employer all day, emphasizing with slender, fluted face wands the four or five expressions that most clearly brought out the emotional state of the particular person. It was an exhausting practice, and one that had taken years to learn. He was, at the time, five months into his unemployment. Mostly, he stayed in bed.

It was morning.

"I'm hungry," Philip said. He was standing next to the bed, clutching his belly theatrically.

"Go down and pour yourself some puffs, chief."

"The puffs are gone."

"I'll make you something later."

"But the food is going away," he said. "There might not be any left later."

"Get dressed," I called out, still half blind from sleep, striking at the air.

"Mother, the food."

I went downstairs. The food was, indeed, going away. The shelves were largely bare — the only indication that food had ever been stored there at all was the mottled, angular stains left by the feet of the plastic containers in which the food was packed. The food that was left was just barely there, dim and shadowy, nearly impossible to hold.

We had been warned about the half-life of food. The Fud Bellows were blamed; we accepted this and forged ahead.

I told my husband that the food was disappearing. I adjusted the pillow under his head and told him that we would be back soon with more. He looked up at me, put a cool hand on my thigh. You need to shave, he said. Please shave before you go.

"You're not going to try it today, are you?"

He said no. He would not try it.

"I put everything away. All the sharp things, the colorful things. Anything that would tempt you."

He said that, yes, he knew. He said he felt safe just curled up in the big bed.

I gathered the razor, gels, limb towelettes, and the coral exfoliant mitt from the low dresser at the opposite end of the bedroom. At the entrance to the water closet I glanced back at him. His head looked small, couched in the center of the quilted orange pillow. He had an expression of false restfulness on his face, the guarded look of someone in the process of constructing an intricate, densely populated society deep inside his body. I try to be careful when I say that this is not the man I knew when we met. I wasn't entirely sure how significantly the person I knew then differed from the other man I found myself next to at the end of each day, the one who remained awake as I slept, slowly chewing dozens of highly involved, conical designs into the bedclothes. He *seemed* different, but sometimes it is the thing that remains most constant that, one day, reveals itself in a strange and terrifying new perspective.

It is difficult to remember with any clarity the time in which we met, partially because I sold a great deal of those memories to buy cloth for Philip's bassinet. We were both young enough to work for Corporation Three, preparing bolts of data-rich burlap for the Hall of the Life Architects. The only memory I can bring up now about those days is the faint image of a man, most likely my husband, moving toward me from across the workshop floor, just a tiny grain of a figure, more than a hundred meters away, bolt scissors slung over his shoulder, kicking up a fine dust. As the man comes closer — I still cannot make out the specifics of his face — his body begins, with each advancing step, to slacken, to fit itself more comfortably into the airspace through which it moves. What at first seems a fleeting, misguided impression gradually gives way to a more fundamental understanding — here is a person undeniably calmed by my presence. It is as close to the idea of an invitation as I have ever seen. Whether or not the man in this memory is my husband, I know that I situated myself in his life throughout the successive years in order to replicate this experience. I'm sure I was able to pull it off more than once, despite what my surviving memories show (hours and hours of nighttime stillness, him lying on his side, breathing delicately into the blue dark; the steamed ring his mug left on the common table; the sweat glistening on his forehead as the doctor slipped Philip's purplish body into his arms for the first time), but I am certain it's been a year or longer since I've seen anything resembling even the faintest degree of interest play itself out on his face. Either that or I've just been less and less capable of projecting an expression of interest into his recessed features.

I cut myself shaving. Actually, it is not accurate to say that I cut myself shaving, because I had not yet begun to shave when I cut myself, and I did not cut my leg but the top of my finger. I had left the razor on the sink before stepping into the deep basin of the shower stall, and when I reached blindly for it from behind the opaque curtain, the top of my left middle finger came off like a pat of butter cleaved from the stick.

I stood in the shower for a good while, holding the newly wounded hand in front of me, tapping with my thumb the lopsided hood of flesh that hung from the tip of my finger. I looked at my hand until it looked like someone else's. Blood welled up in the wound quickly, streaming down my forearm in thin rivulets. The water in the tub went pink and sour. When the wound started to sting I got out and dressed it tightly with toilet paper.

I put Philip in a bright orange snowmobile suit. This was difficult with only one good hand. Philip always wore the snowmobile suit when we went out because it had handles, one on each arm and a big one that doubled as a shoulder strap across the back. We occasionally needed to handle Philip — there was no other way.

"Will we have chocolates?" Philip asked.

"We'll see." There was no difference, nutritionally, between chocolates and, say, broccoli anymore — the withholding of sweets had been stripped of its former power. Most parents persevered, however, believing that there was something instructional about the denial of pleasure. I stood on the fence, admonishing the boy one day and then treating him to heaping bowls of meat cream the next. When I denied Philip's desire, I felt I was doing the right thing, but it also felt good to indulge him in his obsession. I wasn't sure what lesson he was taught as a result, but it seemed to fit in nicely with everything I'd learned about the world in my own childhood.

There were people outside, sitting on the stoop, huddled against one another for warmth. Some of them wore suits made of torn, soiled cardboard. They looked up uniformly as I drew back the screen into its fitted slot. We did not talk to the people, and they did not talk to us. Sometimes, after I'd put Philip on the bus for school, I would scatter hard crusts of bread out into the yard, and they would crouch there, gathering the bits in their gloved hands when they were convinced I was no longer looking.

That day I had no bread. The bread had vanished. I showed them the empty sacks we were bringing to the meat towers. They nodded and made room for us to pass by.

We came to the road, which was glazed over with ice. In its reflection we saw the clouds lurching heavily toward the center of town, noisily grazing the tops of buildings.

"Put on your skates, chief," I said.

"I can run on ice." The boy put forth a small, booted foot, making as if to dash across the slippery surface.

"Philip."

"I can. I can run on ice."

"Do you want me to pick you up by the handle?"

"No, Mother. Don't pick me up by the handle."

"Then you should put on your skates."

The boy collapsed to the ground and lay there for a while, facedown. I turned away, tightening the buckle on my mittens. The left mitten strained against the toilet paper compress, within which throbbed the disabled hand. I could not remember whether gangrene was still a real disease, or what its symptoms were. There would be a blackening, I imagined, a loss of feeling, cramps. I would know when it came.

After a short time, the boy righted himself and slowly put on his skates. We started down the road toward the center of town, toward the meat towers.

"Mother?"

"Yes," I answered.

"Is Father right?"

"Right? In what matter?"

"Right in his head?" The boy looked up at me through the mask of the snowmobile suit, nothing but two distressingly large eyes peering through the embroidered eyeholes. It seemed a strange question. "You mean, is he safe?"

"Yes. Is he safe, or is he getting ready to go away?"

"Philip, why are you talking like this?"

"Sometimes he crawls. On the floor, like a cat. He crawls all around the house and makes cramping noises, like he's trying to poop. Does that mean he is getting ready to go away?"

"Of course not. Perhaps he's just looking for something. Perhaps he's lost something, and he's upset, rooting around in the carpet pile for it. You would be upset if you lost something in the carpet, wouldn't you? I've heard you making some funny sounds, too, young man, down there on all fours, searching for so-and-so's silver missile arm." But even as I said these words I did not believe them — they seemed to appear in the air before us, wispy as tinfoil. I knew that my husband was getting ready to go.

"You're wrong," Philip said, homing in on my carefully concealed doubt. "Cradio's father did the same thing before he went away. He crawled around on the floor in circles, and the circles kept getting smaller and smaller until he was as little as a finger, and then he was gone."

The night before, I woke up to find my husband sitting at the corner of the bed, braiding long strands of the bedclothes into crude rag dolls. He set them on his lap, four in all. "No, I don't want to," he said to them. "I want to stay here." He was holding up his end of a conversation with the stout, featureless figures. "You know I can't stay here. Because you know. If I tell you, everyone will know." In the long pauses between speech he sobbed faintly, jaggedly, shaking the mattress. Each time he shuddered I swear I saw him diminish just slightly in size.

"It wasn't the same. Your father is not going anywhere."

"You're wrong."

To refute him would be to amplify the lie, to give it real weight, so I simply squeezed his hand and we continued on toward the meat towers, the enormous dorsal fins of which loomed ahead in the distance, casting deep, expressive shadows over the road.

"I want him to go," Philip said, huffing pale clouds of condensed breath. "I don't like to have him in that room, always crawling and putting his mouth on my toys."

"I don't want to hear that kind of talk, chief."

"But you tell me to tell you how I'm feeling, no matter what."

"That is not a feeling, chief."

We looked at the apples inside the fruit tent at the base of the meat tower. They were thick and hopeful in our hands; they felt healthy — as if in taking a bite, one could inch closer to some more wholesome state. I let Philip put the apples in the canvas sack, along with the taffy brick and the brittle husks of corn, all painstakingly prepared from various cured meats. Philip was quiet — he put the items into the bag without looking at them, as if to look would be to reveal some fragile, thinly guarded secret.

I put the bag in the brushed aluminum bin of the scale. My finger hummed inside the bloody mitten. My husband — the man who withered away his days in our house, among our toys, our things, shamelessly, openly — had gray eyes, the grayest eyes I'd ever seen. They were like pencil sketches, crude approximations — they were vague and watery enough to take in the whole room at once, which was confusing and frustrating when the one thing I wanted was for him to concentrate on what was going on closest to his face. In some ways, it was easy to understand, already, what he would be like after he was dead.

The apples tumbled around in the sack, shaking the rickety scale, and as it shimmied there next to the cash register I noticed that Philip was gone. The farmer pointed toward the central tower, beneath which several guards had gathered. They cupped their hands to their faces, shouting up to the top, where Philip clung.

"Just let go easily," they called up. "You'll slide down. You won't be hurt."

Philip did not move. He pressed his face into the cool, marbled beef. He was trying to make himself faint. This was what he did instead of crying. He was high up, into the slender neck of the tower, where the meat was frozen, its surface caked over with shining, granular frost.

"What's he doing?" one of the guards asked.

"Might be hungry," the other guard answered. And then he shouted, "Hello? We can give you food down here, buddy. Lots of, like, chocolate for you? Candy canes, fudge bars, the whole shot."

"Your hands are going to freeze right off, champ," the other one joined in. "Or you'll get your hands permanently stuck. We'll have to — I'll tell you, we're going to have to cut big cubes of meat where your hands are, and that meat will be permanently attached to you, so then you'll have to go to school with these, like, big hunks of meat all over your hands."

"No one's going to want that," said the other one.

"No sir. You'll be known as the boy with meat for hands. At school — everywhere. They'll look at you and point and say, 'Hey, isn't that the boy with meat for hands?' And they'll know you're the one because of the big mittens you'll have to wear to cover up the rotting chunks of meat."

"Big mittens, son. Burlap mittens."

Philip responded by burrowing his head farther into the meat. He was up to his ears. Even from where I stood, I could see his little knuckles going white with concentration.

I started toward the tower. I remember thinking clearly that this was a time when something motherly should come to me. I should have been able to conjure up a string of delicate, loving phrases that would turn Philip into an obedient boy, a soft pastry of a child who would loosen his grip just enough to drop contritely to the foot of the tower and bury his small head, fiery with apology, in my lap. But all that came out of me was air, water, heat — the elements of speech without the speech itself, as if my head had not come with a proper instruction manual, or I had not read the one with which it was issued. Suddenly it was as if I no longer had a head at all, as if my body had always held in suspicion the organ that had commanded it with Manichaean accuracy for all these years, and the ugly, perforated case in which it was housed, and a wholesale rejection was, just then, coming to light.

As Philip lost consciousness and began to slide down the slick face of the meat tower, slowly, comically, like a drunk collapsing on a greasy lamppost, the men below advancing with lumbering steps, wielding orange safety blankets and oxygen machines, I thought about my husband, lying there on the bed, how long he had been there, how we would find him, later that day, after having put away the groceries, lying on the bed, in the same position that we'd left him, only smaller, like a doll, his face gruesomely split in half, a tiny, blue handgun nestled in the twisted sheets, still warm, the contents of his head spread out across the pillows like an anatomical diagram — how, even with this degree of detail, the events of his life would remain so distant and abstract to us as never to have really happened at all.

What I wanted, during those years, was to drive a robot. They weren't letting me do that.

"This job does not involve a robot," I told the trembling, wispy human resources clerk at the Ministry of Work and Culture, sliding the brittle manila envelope back across the seafoam Formica surface of the help desk.

"It's as close as we could come, given your circumstances."

"Tooth model?"

"You have very straight teeth."

"Where's the robot in all of this?"

The clerk sat back in his chair reflectively. Behind him was a framed photograph of a group of shirtless men climbing a sheer cliff at sundown, with the inscription T.E.A.M. TOGETHER EVERYONE ACHIEVES MORE. "Geoffrey," he said, "we wouldn't want to mislead you about how endearing we find your crusade. We're actually trying to help you, though it may not seem that way. You're well aware that robots are for boys. Take the tooth model position. Like it."

"I ought to stab you all in the neck," I said. But I took the job anyway, and countless others like it. Finally, I ended up at the Center for Post-Corporate Education, where I taught people how to eat with their whole body.

The problem is that I am a boyish mulatto — I pass for a child, but not for long enough to get a decent job. There is a marker in the grand lobby of the Division of Gradated Employment Services, a red plastic arrow, and like at a child's amusement park ride, nobody even gets to interview for the good jobs unless she can pass safely underneath. I've often fooled them with my height, but something in the way I carry myself has always given away my age, even when I've tried to disguise my behavior with binding nylon tunics and head vests. To put it in the only way it matters, I'm old.

At the center my colleagues and I taught people different techniques of coaching food, getting the best performance out of a meal. This type of eating was called "Eating," and it involved an intricate set of stances that are illegal now. Our goal, stressed in the grueling two-hour instruction tape, was to teach people how to work in the table, the whole room. It was a lifestyle. "When you think about eating," the trainer on the tape said, strolling past a series of staggered food murals, "think about the part of yourself that has to leave to make room for the food coming in. Where does it go? That is the central question. That is when we turn eating into Eating."

The training program was for people who'd reached their Terminal Age Potential, and had been subsequently let go. They were given a voucher by their former employers for a two-month stay at the center. It was a way of burying the rejection, of walking it off, something that people often did after the first part of their life was over.

Our Greeters led the candidates out onto the floor of the loud gymnasium and paired them up with one of us. I was dealt a slight, sooty girl whose nameplate said "Marian: 19 yrs." She was not pretty, but I felt a deep, immediate attraction. Her face was wide and flat, flanged at the ends like a clothes hanger, something familiar you could file yourself away on. She smiled politely as I led her over to our foam practice mat and I saw that a piece of her left front tooth was missing — it was the sort of imperfection that holds all of one's other features hostage. The sudden, panicked manner with which she shut down the expression, before it had fully bloomed, revealed that the defect had marked her for good.

I stood behind her, arms crossed over her abdomen, pressing my palms upward just below her ribs, demonstrating rapid breath technique. I only came up to her shoulders, which made positions such as Filtering the Pool and Attending the Korean Audio Science Museum more challenging than they should have been. Gradually, though, her body yielded to my embrace.

"You've got strong legs," she whispered, unable, in my grasp, to fully enunciate.

"Shhh. No talking," I hissed, irritated and confused that she should comment on the condition of my legs when it was my arms, after all, that were doing all the work.

"I like legs," she said.

I did nothing to engage her further.

"This is such bullshit," she added as we followed the instructions being piped in from the control booth in the ceiling.

"Think of yourselves as big airports," the voice said, "with food planes constantly landing — you've got to get those planes back in the air. How can we get those planes back in the air?"

No one was allowed to communicate at all during the training sessions, but she started asking me things with different outfits she would show up in — one day a bright pink nylon vest, another day brown sweatpants and a yellow scarf. The Greeters frowned upon this. They strongly recommended the hunter green mesh jumpers that everyone else wore, every day, without complaint. Each morning they put her farther and farther back in the snack line as punishment. I was ashamed to be stuck with a miscreant, but also secretly relieved and fascinated. I started answering her queries in the best way that I could, which was to wear a poncho made entirely from the bristled, penetrative half of Velcro.

Three months later, after the graduation ceremonies, I followed her out of the gymnasium. "Say —," I called out, choking on the words. It had been some time since I'd used my face to talk. The muscles in my throat had gone perilously tender from disuse.

She turned, holding her right hand to her throat to indicate her own discomfort.

"I just."

"Yes you. May —"

We strolled, arm in arm, from the center to the tube, trying to avoid conversation, nearly having forgotten what language was for in the first place.

In the tube I wet my pants while she looked at the schedule, but only drop by drop, letting each bit air-dry before moving on to the next.

She'd missed her train, so I took her to my apartment, where we washed down pale green meal tablets with foil sacks of dinner wine. I felt small and far away from her on the couch.

"What — are you?" she said, pointing to my body. It was difficult, in those first days, to understand everything she said — what came out of her was more like a set of breathy, musical notes, whole mouthfuls of them. Pretty, though. I am sure she had the same trouble with my own spittled, mawkish bursts of language. We relied heavily on clothes, sketches, the arrangement of objects in the room to convey meaning.

"No. I'm — I am an older. This person you see — this? I am older than this. Looks? Like."

"Oh. And you — when were you. Terminated?"

"No. Where I work — they know. They — that I am. An old."

She turned to me fully, her voice wavering with tentative, half-turned words. "Geoffrey, what am I supposed — I can't go back to work — I already, went. And they would not? Let me back in."

On someone's last day at one of the corporations, usually his or her nineteenth birthday, the executives throw something called an unwelcoming party, in which the graduating candidate is forced to perform an exit suite on a horned instrument called an octavinet, a relative of the shofar. The performance ends with the removal of the candidate's clothing by his or her coworkers and a subsequent session of intense, bodily humiliation. Live burial in a grain casket was often employed whenever shredded dung was in short supply, before both were outlawed. I imagined Marian's last day — her sudden, awkward shame dramatically exaggerated in the harsh fluorescence of some office lounge while peers looked on, smirking. How she must've looked the next day, showing up, unbidden, loitering at the massive glass doors of the Department of Human Interface

Engineering. I had deftly averted my own unwelcoming from Corporation Two, some twenty years before, by forgetting not to lean too heavily on the flimsy, rusted-out railing of a tiny smoking balcony. It hurt worse than I'd imagined, and one of my kneecaps went permanently numb, but by the time the casts came off, everyone had forgotten I ever worked there.

Marian started to make a face, gnashing her lips like a child cradling some disagreeable food in its mouth.

"Don't — oh, don't. You don't have," I said, drawing her close. I held her head to my chest, away from the mirror on the opposite wall to shield her from her own pale, burst visage.

"What do I — do."

"Let's go — we can go away from here. You can forget. It."

"What do you mean. Go," she said, straightening up a little.

"I'm not — that is — we could easily. That is, leave. On a flying object — one of those —"

"Airplane."

"Yes."

"Oh. I would very. Much like that," she said, grinding a mashed tissue into one eye socket.

"Right then."

"Will it actually. Leave — the ground because? I can't leave the ground because? Of a fake lung. A plastic lung. That will inflate in the — air."

I booked us on an ocean cruise instead. We would pass through Oceans Three and Four over the course of two weeks in a luxury vessel, the Travel Administrator informed me, one of the large, air-buoyed ones with wide glass fins.

"Which package would you prefer?" she asked.

"Whatever costs the most of — that object drawn from an

employer, a paper item. Colorful — that is — how does one call this?"

"Money. The one that costs the most money?" answered the small, distant voice through the speech bead.

"Yes. Please remove as much money as possible. From myself."

"This is truly — it's something I'll never forget," she said when we saw the vessel for real. Holding a wide-brimmed hat close to her head against the gusting bay breeze, she ushered me on with great enthusiasm.

"You're walking me too fast," I said, stumbling to keep pace.

"That's the point, dear." Her sentences were getting more elaborate and vivid. My own speech had always left something to be desired, so often had I abused it with silence. Even more so with Marian, though — I dreaded saying something that might offend her, terrified that she might simply disappear in retaliation.

Neither of us had ever been on a cruise — I hadn't ever had a proper vacation before, save for the series of private debasements that passed as family trips. The idea of a cruise was appealing. It was the only way you could get far away from people and stay there, suspended in the amniotic grace of the ocean.

We stood at the guardrail as the vessel pulled away from the harbor. Surprisingly, people had actually shown up to wave at us from the docks.

"What it must have been like for people simply to have gone off on a trip," Marian said, watching as the land became a distant smudge on the horizon. "Just to go, you know?"

"Aren't we doing that?"

"This? This is what we do so that we can forget that we can't do what we used to do."

The vessel hit full speed, rising slightly above the water. I crashed into Marian, clutching wildly at her hips as I collapsed. "You're such a dear," she shouted over the ocean spray, petting my head as I knelt before her.

The first night we were herded into a narrow lounge. There was a magic show, in which a man in a white mask pulled cards from the air. From our vantage point his secrets were revealed. The rest of the audience sat mesmerized. They were old, most of them in their seventies. "They want to be tricked," Marian said.

Later, we went up on the sun deck, but there was no sun, only the dim yellow light given off by the incandescent bulbs that ran along the perimeter of the vinyl buffet table canopy and the infinite deadness of the night sky. Somewhere in the ship, a band was playing old songs — we heard tender strains of something drifting up through the narrow mouth of the staircase. I drew Marian close to me, turning her body so that we could assume the Eating stances that had brought us together. We fell into a rapturous, tandem dance.

"This is," I said, pressing her as close to my body as I could, "you are so much of a surprise — I didn't think. What I did think was that — you were — so young. We could help each other be together, couldn't we?" The band finished the number. A great crowd of people applauded, and they started in again with another bleating, primitive waltz. In several of the most important ways, I had the distinct sensation of already having attached Marian to the rest of my life.

"Oh my God," she whispered between sharp, heavy breaths. "Oh Jesus God." Standing behind her, I did not see when she started to cry, but felt her body sag and lurch.

"What — do you?"

"I need to. Get back —" It was difficult to tell whether this last fragment was a proclamation or a directive. She slipped out of the Eating stance we'd attained, Pride of the Alaskan Pipeline, and broke away to the stairwell. I followed her into the belly of the vessel, back to our cabin, which looked, suddenly, as though it had been made with a crayon and a napkin. She was sitting on the bed, satin dress half off, hands pressed to her face.

"Jesus, what's — wrong?"

She did not look at me, but slowly capsized onto the bed, like the victim of a slow-motion shoot-out.

"Marian. What's —"

There was a television monitor bolted high on the wall opposite the bed, which broadcast the view from the bridge all day and all night. It was what we had in place of a window. The screen was a deep black then, save for a single, tiny string of bulbs that ran down the middle of the vessel, lights that hardly put a dent in the night.

She took her hands from her face, where mascara had pooled in heavy, expressive crescents. "Geoffrey, I — you're an old person. Your skin is so — it's like a sequoia — you're like an antique chicken. I'm sorry — you're very kind and I might even love you in some awkward manner, but I'm sickened by the presumption your body makes to the world. When you hold me, I think of my father, of the brutal Indian rope burns he would give me during summer break at night after my mother passed out. He'd press himself up behind me, and it was like being lowered into a tub of thick dough. I let him do it again and again because I knew that someday I was going to be one of him — my body was going to be wrecked and pinched off like an ancient, desiccated fruit. I felt as if I needed practice at being sick with myself. The sickness of it got inside me — whenever they were away, I tried to make myself old, brushing school glue on my face and arms and letting it dry there. I would sit in front of my bedroom mirror for hours, masturbating to the image of my own wasted body. But now it's actually happening to me. Here, this boat — I'm already there. This is old. I'm going to be old. So soon I can already feel it. I don't want to be an old person, Geoffrey. I don't want to be an old person. Jesus." She started to sob uncontrollably — the whole room seemed to shake with each violent contraction of her body.

"Please oh please, Marian, don't — you shouldn't —"

"Just, just go."

"You want me to —"

"Go."

I had never been so close to a person in this condition. Most of the people I knew who didn't want to become old had simply killed themselves. Myself, I tried to but was unable to fully remove myself from the act. I kept making incisions and then reneging, so that after two hours or so, with blood everywhere in my small, dingy kitchen, I gave up and fell into a deep sleep on the floor.

I left Marian in the cabin, curled around herself, clutching a fistful of toilet paper. She looked like a stuffed puppet, something I could fit inside a cereal bowl. Her face was white, charged with cold sweat. It was true that she was going to be old — there was little I could do.

I was alone on the sun deck. The sound the brackish pool water made as it lapped gently against the porcelain ledge merely intensified the terror that the ocean invoked. That there was a start and a finish to it was inconceivable, but there *was* a start and a finish, surely, because how could something just be there, infinitely? There in the darkness, in the cold, whole periods of my own life made themselves suddenly and shamelessly apparent, but they, too, were always the middle part, never a beginning or ending. I remembered having been an altar boy, for instance, but could not remember when I had stopped being one. Did I draft a letter of resignation, or had I simply stopped showing up? Because, surely, some church representative would have called my parents, or would they? And what had happened to those hours I had unmoored myself from? What part of me started there, in that dark hole I had ripped for myself?

I stayed on the deck throughout the night. The world around the boat was the darkest, densest possible thing. It just ended there over the railing. There ought to have been some lights blinking somewhere, if only to defeat the suggestion that people had not been out there before. I thought about the darkness as a sort of blindness, but it was really nothing like blindness, which is when there is actually something in front of you to see.

At dawn, the sky turned brown, then yellow, then brown again. The elderly passengers began lining up at the buffet table, cupping their plastic bowls eagerly while staff members carefully served steaming ladlefuls of cream of beef. If I'd been able to drive a robot, I would be far away from this place, sailing quietly above some heaving city, hovering over all of the pointless, overwrought lives metastasizing below in crowded rooms.

Marian came up beside me.

"What are you —"

She was feeling better, and suggested that we sit in the stern of the vessel, as far back as possible, where there couldn't be any more people.

There were some deck chairs, and a model of an old captain's wheel. The sun was half out, mincing behind an obsidian cloud mass. We stood at the rail for a while, leaning far out enough so that the only trace of the vessel we could see was a small, tattered flag hanging off the back. Marian's face was puffy and splotched. I put my arm around her waist. The ship cut a deep, ragged swath through the water. We felt its motion most clearly there, felt it go up, then down. On each downstroke, the ship seemed to say, "Damn."

We sat. "This doesn't mean I don't hate this, every bit of it," she said, reaching over for my hand. An older couple came up right next to us, a man and a woman. The man had on a captain's outfit, bought from the gift shop, complete with a hat and false beard. He handed the woman a camera. "Try and get some of the ocean in the background," he told her. She fingered the buttons on the camera while he took the wheel, posing stoically, stiff-armed. The woman edged herself against the metal stairwell. We watched the whole thing.

"Let's not stay out here long," Marian said, and I agreed. It hardly mattered what we would miss by going inside; there wasn't a trace of land in sight. The man and the woman took their photographs and left. I chose a spot in the ocean with my eyes, a swirling eddy, bright with foam, and focused on it as we bore on through the morning. Marian slipped a foot out of her sandal and ran it over my calf. I watched the little eddy until it was nothing, until it was water again.

We were in the sky tent, harvesting air.

"Push off, guv'ner," said the terse, black-veiled Minister, and the hard, black cloud lurched underneath us. "Push off, push off. On to the next we go." The bellows heaved with the sudden current, swelling with the dilapidated gusts of colored air we gathered into the tent.

Chunk finished his cigarette and tossed it off the side of the cloud. We leaned on our harvesting wands — long poles with soft, absorbent swab tips — and watched the tiny embers of the butt sail away from us toward the awkward, disheartening cityscape, a cheesy gridwork of dilapidated factories and town houses that from our vantage point seemed only to map out the hysterical flight pattern of the people who threw themselves into it on a daily basis. We were intractably beside ourselves.

I'd lived in two of the houses down there, when "down there" was actually a place I lived. I willed the cigarette's trajectory down the chimney of the first house I'd lived in, a building that still paid lip service to my first and only husband. Down the chimney and into the chemical vase, I prayed, where, if I were lucky, the resultant flash fire would scorch beyond recognition not only his rueful face but also the couch where I'd combed his hair each morning, the hallway mirror against which I'd pressed him countless times, plugging his tight fissure with two trembling fingers, and the collection of lurid photographs we'd made in the dusky light of a drive-thru arch — pictures that failed, like everything else we did, to amount to anything but evidence of drunken hubris. He was a straw-armed man, willfully spindly, who made his presence known only when he was not around, so that in living with him I was most alone when we shared the same room, sucked on the same withered airspace.

The second house, my first wife's, would be far enough away to survive the blast.

"Chirrup, chirrup." This was Wendell. He had on a Dutch shirt and slight, noisome huaraches.

Chunk cursed in a low voice, ducking behind the bellows.

"I have nothing to say to you, Wendell." I had nothing to say to Wendell.

Wendell was the new husband to my first wife, the first male husband she'd had. He was chubby, his skin stretched tight like a plastic garbage bag. I thought about her hand on his chest, how small it would appear, how dark, next to this man's heaving whiteness.

"I can put some words in your mouth for you," he said. "I have some spare lines in the speech tube." He patted his lumbar satchel. Wendell was a person who required some sort of dialogue to make it through a day. Most people did, especially in the sky tent, where the only other thing to do was watch the crawling progression of the dirty earth below. I avoided conversation not for what it did to me but for what it did to *them,* how improbably vulnerable it rendered anyone who gave it a shot.

"Whatever makes you feel better," I said, and knelt to receive the mouthpiece, because what else does one do in circumstances such as this? Why should I have denied this man yet another chance to dangle his trumped-up life over my own?

He inserted the mouthpiece. I could taste the lives of men and other women, could sense, though surely it must have been my own creation, the pungent, confectionary muck of my first wife's slobber, worked permanently into the chomped, matted tooth grooves.

I let my mouth go slack. He toggled the twin sticks of the remote, filling my oral cavity with rich, suggestive air. My face said the things he wanted it to.

"Chirrup, chirrup." This was his steel lung, which whirred and gasped as the multitudes of tiny cogs toiled away, generating a false, tittering air of hope. "I'm glad, you know, that we could talk," he said.

My mouth was limp, numb.

It was time to get back to work. Wendell coiled the apparatus and slipped it back into his bag. "Thanks. I —"

"No. Don't," I said. I was drooling evenly into my palm. "Just tell me — can she walk?"

"She can write and hold a cup. She can look at things. We're working on a puzzle together."

"A puzzle? With your salary you can't do better than that?"

"Afraid not, ma'am. She has to *want* to walk first. She has to develop that first, well, spark, you could say. That motivational, you know, thing."

"There's no reason for her to walk."

"Well, no," Wendell said, partly to his own chest. He spoke softly, solemnly, as if he were trying to mat down the wiry hairs on his torso with soothing words.

He took his position toward the stern with the other young men. We stirred the thin air with the staffs, coating the swabs with a coarse sheet of oxygen. We coaxed the air down into the citybound transport valves, our ululating wands like the shuddering cilia of some great animal.

I had a letter in my pocket. It said "Dear Prell." This was my ex-wife's first name. "Dear PRELL," it said again — I wanted the name to spring out from the page, to molest her sensibility, to hazard the slightest ripple in the hazy periphery of her life. Under her name I drew a picture of a small animal, a figure that, drawn by a more experienced hand, might begin to resemble a tapir but that in my own curlish, misinformed penmanship looked like a mangy dog. I did not know what this meant at the time — the act of sketching was nothing more than a way to calm my nerves as I fashioned the note, a method of maintaining some sort of bodily restraint. But over days the animal started to mean something else entirely. Smudged haphazardly from pocketwear, the creature became animated, the sharp fur along its back bristling in preparation for some imminent attack.

"DEAR PRELL," it said underneath the crude thumbnail image, "When I look down I will always see the top of your head, the feature you let me maul most frequently. I can remember each divot with a phrenologist's precision. Remember how I wept when they finally smoothed it all over? How I held your tender head in the recovery room, knowing, even then, even after the accident, with your face like a blunt mallet, that I would never fully rid myself of you? I will admit now what I would not admit then, that it was my fault, that I was tipsy and that I told you I knew how to drive the pram out of spite. But the fog that night, the animals in the road, the half-naked farmer — how could I have planned that? Please, understand at least that much.

"Your head, now, from up here, couldn't be measured in pixels. A grain of sand would crush you, Prell. You feel, nightly, the tugging, insistent member of a man straining against the small of your back, when my only mistake was actually leaving when I finally got the idea to do so. I am still here, Prell, PRELL, groaning with fossilized desire. You shit."

I looked the letter over once more. I hadn't said anything more or less than that I was unprepared to make any statements on my own behalf. I was a career coward, unfit for the rigor of even the most childish, underdeveloped day. The sky stopped for a break. Chunk went for his cigarette box. I tied the note to a small brown pebble of hard air, poked a small hole in the cloud, and dropped it right through.

I made them for the Museum of Real Estate and Finance. They sent me out with a special microphone and a tape deck. People wanted to know what kind of lives had molted and languished in the places where they would like to file away their own blustery, overwrought experiences. I'd spend a day or two in different areas of a house, using the long, fluted horn of the microphone to record the billion fluttering tones, the way different angles of sunlight on the walls colored reflections, memories of footsteps embedded deep within the wide slats of the floor, the places where the last people who lived there grieved and sprawled, shed tiny, creped flakes of life. On a certain frequency, I could pick up fragments of a conversation between two people who had perhaps long lost touch with each other by then. Another frequency might unveil the stuttering wow and report of a coital episode occurring in the kitchen. You could modulate the pitch so that even the soiled breath of the couple was audible from inside the oven. The bathroom was a particularly fertile site. I would sit cross-legged on the floor of a house's bathroom for hours, listening carefully through headphones at the timbre of the different silences, how they cascaded into and breached one another. We used to think that houses had no memory at all. But now we understand.

Though it was not my job, I would sometimes go around a certain house, fixing up some of the minor imperfections — a dangling shade, perhaps, or an unhinged door. Who could *not* fix something that was just lying there, broken to the world? How could you just leave something out like that, hanging like some fibrous, gangly appendage?

I worked part-time so that I could spend the rest of my day listening to houses that were currently inhabited. My wife's home, for instance, was a place I was very familiar with. She brought a child and a waffle iron into our relationship; I brought nothing but a lifetime of pouting and relentless self-indulgence. Nevertheless, I was given a set of keys to her place and permission to use the bed and washroom, but not a towel or soap. "For a person that has never heard of self-reliance . . . ," she'd say, face brought into sharp relief by some base cosmetic arrangement. Consequently, I washed during the day, using a dingy, thirdhand set of linens I kept in a plastic bag under the tub, long after she had trudged off to the job that rubbed her bricked, shuttered life away, paycheck after paycheck.

She had lots of little things around — a smirking, Bakelite cat clock, two tall reed baskets of seemingly foreign origin, a lone ski pole with the word *champ* written in squidgid, blocked Magic Marker script — objects that stood for various times and places in her life, the relevance of which she vigilantly kept from me. When I sensed one in a room, I would check it with the house machine and, sure enough, all kinds of sound would come rushing out of it.

I listened to her things for hours while she was at work, carefully running over each surface with the slim, troweled orifice of the microphone, scanning the frequencies for some meaningful tone. On hot, dry days swatches of fabric tended to surrender the most vivid signals. At times, the sound was clear enough to evoke a kind of sightfulness. One morning a nettled tuft of hair brought about a striking tableau of her child, Janet. She was just starting to walk. There were some sounds of her feebly traversing the corner of an apartment that I had never seen or even heard of but that had very nice things in it, much nicer than the things we had in our house. On another frequency I could hear the child handling some plastic figures and blocks, trying to paste together some sort of world out of the cheap talismans. Her head shook like one of those big-headed figurines with springs for necks. By the time I started wedging myself into her life, the girl could already put on her own shoes and say things like "We're going faster."

The end of each day had the habit of getting right up in my face, with little or no advance warning. I locked down the house I was sounding — a massive, interbred structure buttressed by haughty, overdesigned columns and balustrades — and hauled the tapes back to the Museum of Real Estate and Finance. The foreman had a disagreeable face and body, as if it had been preempted by terminal indecision at an early stage.

"What there — you?" he asked from behind the marquee. He was blind by choice, just like my father.

"A couple of instructive loops. Some business about a fancy dress, a boating accident, Ibiza."

"Clean?"

"So far."

"So far, so far."

It was a job that did what I wanted it to. It stayed wherever I put it. Where I lived, though, was massive and untenable, an emotional dumping ground — a house whose thin meniscus trembled and brimmed with discontent.

The relationship my wife and I kept taking stabs at didn't slip through my fingers so much as level itself sloppily against them. We were still passing back and forth a virus I had picked up years before. It became part of what we did together — the life we fostered in lieu of a child of our own.

I was rarely satisfied with what I had heard in our house, so I continued on through the bedroom every morning, taking samples from anything that resonated. Each fragment of my wife's memory left a hole where another one started. One by one they began to pull me along into the other side of her life, the part that happened before I had started greedily busting it up at every available opportunity. I'm not sure what I expected to find — probably some clear confirmation that the time in which she had known me was intense enough to invalidate her past experience. I did not know the people that had trespassed into her life before me, and was interested in what they had to say for themselves.

One morning, after a few cursory passes around the bedroom, I found exactly the kind of thing I was looking for. In one of her closets, wedged in behind a box of china, was a red plastic sandal. It resonated at a near perfect B-flat, though the signal was tainted by frequent, intense arpeggiated bursts of vibrato. The sound was my wife, before she was my wife or even a person I had ever known, sitting next to a baby pool, inside of which were the kid, Janet, and her father. I had met this man a few times in real life — he was the kind of thing you'd expect to see — underbaked, corn shaped, toothy. He made a lot of money in the city designing cloud advertisements, so that everything he said was either from a commercial or soon to be one. He was already into his twenties, and hadn't yet been unwelcomed. My wife, this person she was, you could see she was trying to hold things together. She held Janet's hand to keep her balance and poured water over her back with a small plastic cup.

I didn't like what the sound was doing to my body — I went cold, and there was a spot in the center of me that glowed like a car lighter, but it didn't stop me from listening. I held a finger over the teardrop-shaped mute button in case there was something I didn't want to hear. There were lots of things that I might never want to hear. When I was a schoolboy I took this girl up to the city to make a dirty movie. Only I wanted it to be a silent film. I told her she wasn't allowed to make a sound — not even the rustle and bond of her skirt and top as she peeled them slowly from her body, a noise that I can only refer to as "stez." I put a belt around her neck and worked at her pasty, splotched body from behind. The headboard kept banging into the wall, so I had to stuff some pillows in the crevice between. She parried and lurched like an understudy for some lanky, newborn animal, skinny legs canted in the hideous lamplight. Watching that tape now, after about ten years, is a shameful and embarrassing procedure. Seeing myself swagger around in silence, holding my breath, cock dipped and pitted, my hands in places that hands shouldn't go, is like having your own worst time in your life and someone else's all at once.

The family sat in the pool for a long time. This father had a little squirt toy and started to use it on the child and my wife. "Honey, she seems thirsty," my wife said to the father. He turned and squirted my wife's upper thigh, marking a trail up toward her crotch. He stretched out his arm, holding the nozzle of the gun over her midriff, soaking the entire region. There was something sad and groping about the sound of the water splashing against her beige stove pants — a lostness, the collapsing wheeze of a flaccid and forgettable overture. My wife only looked at him. The father continued spraying her crotch, grinning like the wide, unseemly grille of a truck. I had never heard of someone so completely oblivious to his surroundings.

But I promised myself, there in the bedroom, sound machine in my lap, that I would not malign the father. I would keep my feelings to myself, where nobody has any business with them anyway. I don't like it when people can tell what I'm feeling, and I don't like it when they try. That is why I don't say anything to anyone. My wife preferred it this way — she could get more done.

This business with the pool continued for some time, with these characters who had barnstormed the periphery of my life sitting around in the heat with pinched, dumbfounded expressions. I'd had enough, and put everything back the way I had found it.

The house I went to that day was loud, filled with the dull, inlaid memories of a hundred lives. The clients would be disappointed in the reels — none of these people were especially upstanding or even had anything of interest to contribute to a conversation. Light hit the walls and floor in strange, unanticipated waves of grief. The bedroom keened softly the whole time I was there. Ancient prints of bodies lolled and shifted in the adjoining hall. The tone of the place was marbly, clotted. This would drive the price down considerably, although the tub made an exquisite sound. It was the centerpiece of the whole place, probably because nobody had chosen to mark it with the indelible effluvium of her life.

The foreman asked me what I'd gotten.

"You know when people ask you to think of a bad thing and multiply it by ten?"

I handed him the envelope with the reels. He felt at it for a long, self-absorbed moment, speculating on the relative value of the contents.

"This fucks us."

I told him that the house would never be sold, that the whole place was caked over. He filed away the envelope in one of the big diagnostic machines. I went out and had a cigarette. The day, with all its bitter, ridiculous interstices, had been killed.

The next morning that unnamable sense, the thing that made me take out the microphone the day before, was back. My wife was up again, in the bathroom, preparing her face for work. The girl had wandered in during the night and was sleeping crosswise on the bed. I held my stomach, thinking about the father, that place she had made in the world that was now gone. Where was I, then, on the morning they squatted in that cheap pool?

How would my own life appear on that day from someone else's perspective, from *his* perspective? How did I tick away those hours, useless and alone in South City? Could I have those gestures, that day, back again?

I got in my car and circled the neighborhood a few times, waiting for my wife to leave. Everything was curiously dead in the sharp streets. When I was sure the house was empty, I went back and turned on the machine. There was a narrow crack in one of the floorboards, from which I extracted the yellowed flap of an envelope, glue and all. Something about the offhand way it had been discarded drew me to it. Under the slim trowel of the microphone's horn it seemed to shimmy and buck. It took longer than usual to draw out a signal — what did come was brittle and insubstantial. I was hard-pressed for detail and clarity. By interpolating the middle C with a B-flat, though, I was able to conjure up the sound of the father. He stood naked to his socks in a dim, brownish room, talking to a couple of people sitting on the couch. It came at me fiercely, out of the late morning. His body, barely distinguishable from the washed-out, underlit background, was thin and frail, and the way he moved suggested the palsied antics of a small boy. I couldn't follow the thread of his talk — he said things like "The greatest fucking year I'd like to fuck." Occasionally the noise would list toward the couch, where the other couple was laid out, shamefully distended and half dressed. The father danced by the empty cavity of a fireplace, the bowed tine of his dick swaying, half erect.

I listened, cradling the lozenge-shaped recording deck like a tender football. Forgive me for saying that it was something that couldn't *not* be heard. It flickered before me, monstrous and immense, the realization of some deep, long-choked fear. Here was the soft, purloined limb that had held my wife's time and energy hostage for nine years, braying at the entrance to her unwitting, shadowy womb. Something inside me broke like a glass vial. I got it all over myself.

I sat there in the same fashion as, probably, my wife had when she was taking in this particular sound. And what about her life? What was she doing in this scene — how could she have stood for it, any of it? Is this what they did back then, night after night, squirming nakedly in each other's spaced-up Western Coastal apartments?

Predictably enough, my wife showed up then, having forgotten the kid's day-care bag. We regarded each other for some time, the silence of the room interrupted only by the inane, periodic bursts of the child's father. She made a series of high-pitched, desultory sounds, on the pretext of making language. I had nothing to apologize for, never having promised her anything by way of personal consideration. She took a step forward. I put the machine on the bed and grabbed my jacket. She assumed, I think, that we would have something to say, but I pushed past her in the narrow hall and took the stairs all the way down.

Outside, it was bright, unforgivably so. I could hardly see to my car. And what then? Should I say that I got in and drove off, smoking one cigarette after another, lining them up end on end until I was all of the way out of that life? Because what happened was that I stayed there, with those people, for another three and a half dreadful, thoroughly forgettable years in the way that we best know how to make ourselves feel welcome wherever we'd least like to be.

Year 51

Fragment

Did you pack your ointment, dear?" I called across the hood of the car.

The Child Harvesting counselor had just called to confirm our slot at 15:30. It was conception day.

Chu Su gave me a look, so I went and got the ointment myself.

The drive took half a day. "The second half will be better," I told her. She just looked straight ahead at the road, her face blank as chalk.

The building that housed the Ministry of Child Harvesting had just recently been converted from the Ministry of Adhesives and Wood. The whole place smelled like pine sap. Good, though. A fresh scent.

The counselors guided us down a long hallway to a white room with glittering, quilted walls. At the center of the room was a small vehicle for two. The seats faced each other, one with a recessed area for the man and the other with a single curved prong for the woman. Rising from the center of the vehicle was a steel post from which branched two sets of handlebars, and where the handlebars joined the post there were two monitors.

This was a conception simulator, the counselors told us. They told us to disrobe and promptly left the room.

"I didn't think it would be quite so — I just feel a bit empty,"

Chu Su said. We knew little about the procedures involved beforehand, only that a child would be legally assigned to us at the end of the third trimester.

"Let's just get it done quickly. If the brochure is correct, the rest is much easier and more pleasant."

We got naked. She was gorgeous when dressed, but without clothes she was like a packet of sugar with toothpicks for limbs. Thin, but in the wrong way. I wondered how the trimestral simulation vests would even fit on her. Probably they'd have to sew a custom model.

"Stop looking at me like that," she said. "Your body is nothing exceptional, either, Mr. Fake Foot."

Yes, the fake foot. The real one I'd lost in War 5. I'd gotten it caught between two rocks during a decisive retreat. "Either we cut off the foot or you die," the captain said, and before I could respond they'd severed the foot at the ankle with a pair of bone-cutting shears. I went back to the spot some months later, after we'd retaken the stretch of land, but the foot was gone.

We got into the vehicle. When our genitals had warmed the receptacles sufficiently, the monitors clicked on and the vehicle started to drift across the floor on a cushion of air.

A featureless head came up on the monitor. "Welcome. Thank you for investing in the future of our great nation. We have successfully determined your racial makeup. You may now select an egg cluster from one of the following regions: Pusan, Seoul, Cheju, Pyongyang."

I looked up. Chu Su was weeping, streaming silent tears.

"Does it hurt?" I asked, reaching out to touch her arm over the handlebars. The voice on the monitor said, "Please do not remove your hands from the handgrips at any time during this simulation."

The vehicle did slow doughnuts in the center of the concrete floor.

"No," she said. "I can't feel anything at all."

The Tins

They have taken the joy of eating from us, and so we sit at table, hands folded in prayer, each in personal cardboard food booths. At the beginning of our meal, the signal is given. Elaine inserts the corn cob. William, with half-palsied face, picks at his beefsteak. "No more of that," cries Mother. "No more — we will have no more of that," she calls from her booth. Father, having come to us by means of a remote-control device, slouches in his chair, head in hands. Perhaps he does not belong to us. The twins feed each other dense gray portions of mashed potato, pasting the material to each other's face and forehead. "No more of that — children." Mother will use the wooden spoon, she warns them. The portions, delicately and lovingly arranged on every plate, will taste no different than on other nights. Meals arrive at our doorstep in heavy tins. Instructions are that each family member assist in the meal. William will help stir. Elaine needs a phone book to stand on. I will sift flour from a metal can with a trigger. Look, a tasty dip can be made with sour cream and onion soup. Mother tucks the meat, garnishing it with cherries and pineapple rings.

Novelty of Heat

The joy of eating taken from us, we are allowed to play in the yard. William, this time, is the German. We each break into a rapid, awkward gait, scattering across the lawn. Elaine crouches behind the hedge. The twins have not learned the rules. William is gaining on them. I have climbed into the high branches of the sycamore tree, where the animal qualities of children are most apparent. This section of the yard is made up entirely of smells. William falls ass-backwards, wheezing, the wind knocked out of him. A truck rolls down the street, selling cupped ice. Summer will pass in this way, each night progressively longer, more dissonant, objects lurching in the sky overhead.

The Hard Candies

The joy of eating is gone. Mother, having taken the Germans for a walk, washes her face and hair in the kitchen sink. We are not to look. Father works alone in the forbidden room. It is conjectured that he has been to war. Elaine shows me her secret, a cache of brightly colored hard candies she hides behind the porch steps. She sucks on one and begins to cry. Everything is about as useful as water now.

Into Her Mouth

Eating, that joy in which we have taken part for as long as we can remember, has been revoked. Father is outside, wielding the lawn mower in concentric squares. William, who has been punished, sits alone in his room in a chair by the window, diagramming the behavior of birds. Elaine is out with friends. I am sitting down to a bowl of ice and a fresh comic book. It is cool here in the dark kitchen. Summer, as reported, has been the worst season for food. Dirt has a taste, it is reported. The suggestion is that one mix small amounts of dirt into one's meal. Mother, in her garden, gingerly inserts a finger into her mouth.

Joust

Each of us, in turn, recalls the joy of eating, now lost to us. William has been fighting with the other boys. They wear cloth helmets and carry long wooden poles for jousting. The goal is emasculation. They can be heard in the streets before dark, charging at one another fiercely. An ice cone truck passes. Mother sets her magazine down, neck craned in the direction of the window. On television, hands hold up black holes where food was once inserted. Elaine has locked herself in an upstairs closet, where she says there is "another kind of air."

Joy of Sleep, Interrupted

Because the joy of eating has been lost, we are huddlers. We are loitering in our own lives. William's bed-wetting incidents have

increased in number and intensity. Father finds tiny holes bored
into the mattress and inserts a diode into the head of William's
penis to shock him awake next time.

The Back of Abraham

Eating, the joy of which has been wrested from us, becomes difficult. Out behind the pond Peter has found a can with something in it. Half of us are wearing ornate Indian headgear. Jill
shakes the can, putting it to her ear. "I can hear the heart of it
moving." There is a box with mason jars filled with dark, pulpy
objects soaking in their own fluids. Abraham opens a jar and
picks out a wedge of something that looks like a small lung. "It
is softer than you would expect," he says. "Less substantial.
Messy, like a wet genital." He holds it to his mouth. For a long
moment nobody says anything. "No," he says, lips slick and red
from handling, "I'm afraid not." Some pioneer from the other
side of town shoots an arrow from over the hill, which pierces
Abraham's shoulder. Those of us who do not run don't know
what to do, either. Abraham hunches over, the arrow quivering
in his back.

Joy of Eating, v. 2

Hot fresh-baked corn cakes! Spoonfuls of homemade apple-
sauce!

For the Memory of Food

They fly over us in great planes and drop pamphlets: "For the Memory of Food." Some people in the town have fled over the hill and off into another town. The houses where they lived stick out like buck teeth along the street, busted into and painted over in red. Peter has left with his family, all of them taking only what they could carry. Those of us who remain have satisfied ourselves with the carving of immense, ornate ice sculptures, displayed in our front yards for the children to come and lick. One morning, by cosmic fluke, everyone makes swans.

The Hands

What a joy, to eat. We find ourselves in the kitchen, wandering, fingering cardboard cartons stacked away in high cabinets and filled with cornstarch and water. Whatever it is we did not want to become, we have become. I meet Father one night in the hallway, his face riddled with pasty crumbs from a paper sandwich. Shamefully, we hold our places there in the cold, blue light, regarding each other. His father was a Methodist preacher — he has the same tendency to turn red. "There, there, now, off to bed with you," he says, holding out large, paddle-like hands, the kind that might get you ready for a smack. He hooks them under my arms and lifts. I can feel how heavy I must be, slouched there over his shoulder. On my pajamas cloned cowboys rope pastel steers in unison, the way you seem to stay a certain age forever.

Pembroke got a box in the mail. A big box, wrapped in brown paper, about twice the size of a human head.

"What's that?" said Clay, rising halfway from the couch, as if a lady had entered the room.

"Nothing."

"Come on."

Pembroke hugged the box sheepishly in the open doorway. He seemed to disappear behind it. "It's nothing."

They had been sitting in front of the entertainment center before the box had come. There was a program on about how horses make love. Clay had brewed up some egg salad for Pembroke in the food-o-rator and poured some hard puffs for himself. The food lay strewn out on the coffee table, half eaten.

Clay stood there, hesitating over the couch, looking at Pembroke's box.

"Come on."

"Dude, it's nothing."

Pembroke took the box into his bedroom and shut the door.

Clay followed a few steps behind, lingering in the empty hallway.

.   .   .

There were two ways the pill could be taken — as a regular pill
or as a suppository, and Pembroke did not like the taste of these
things, though they made him feel as if he were a soldier in one
of the great armies. He and a few of the other boys crowded
into the tiny rest-room stalls of the abandoned comedy club and
squatted. The pills fizzed pleasantly, like Alka-Seltzer, only bigger — an armada of Alka-Seltzer. Pembroke had brought a rubber bib to wear beneath his underwear, only because sometimes
the stuff would run out of you before it got a chance to take
effect, making both a stain there on the worst place to have a
stain and also all of the, like, drugness leaking away into your
pants.

Pembroke's father owned the comedy club. The club was
abandoned primarily because Pembroke's father was dead.

They started down the steps to the basement, where there
were more boys and a few girls.

"I can't believe this is where you were conceived," said
Thorpe, pointing to a portrait of a group of dogs playing bil-
liards. "This place is funny as hell."

"I got one of those helmets," said Pembroke.

"What kind of helmet?" Thorpe replied, leading the way
down the narrow stairs.

"That kind where you can talk to your past."

"I would not want to talk to my past. No one is even doing
that anymore."

"Well, I am," he said, more to himself than to Thorpe, who was far ahead by now, bounding down the rickety stairwell.

They opened the door to the men's dressing room. Everyone was laid out on couches, barely conscious. The room was cluttered with broken stage props — a purple throne, a stuffed dog, two giant plastic asses. A group of thin, pasty girls looked up as Thorpe, Pembroke, and the rest entered. "I'm going to get in that," said Thorpe, and Pembroke thought he was talking about Joy Pfeiss or at least Crystal Carpenter. But Thorpe started to climb into the clothes dryer instead. He was the kind of thin where you could see his bones moving around underneath the skin as if he were concealing another person, and you wondered what it would take for that person to tear right through.

Thorpe was trying to get himself inside the machine, legs first. The suppositories had made him unsteady — his limbs banged against the corrugated steel drum of the dryer, but before anyone could dissuade him he was all the way in, curled up like one of those Russian space monkeys they shot off in the olden days.

"Shut it," he called from the chamber. "Shut the door to this thing and let it go."

Some of the boys and girls in the room had stopped petting each other in order to get a better look at Thorpe, but no one made a move toward the machine. "Shut it," Thorpe called again, banging on the walls of the drum with his fists for emphasis. "Start me up. I'm going to leave this place. Is somebody going to help me here?" The room grew quiet.

Bluth mumbled, "Thing takes quarters, man."

"Quarters? Jesus, I'll give you all quarters." Thorpe, because of the way he had stuffed himself inside the dryer, could not look directly at any of them. He could just sort of shout at his own chest. This pinched off his vocal cords in such a way that what came out was more of a high-pitched whisper than anything else, as if he'd inhaled a canister of helium. "Maybe you don't understand. I am flying out of here, and whoever puts a quarter in this machine will not get their ass kicked on my way out. How's that for a motherfucking bargain?"

Pembroke inched backward to the trophy cabinet, where all his father's awards were kept. He had gotten Thorpe hurt a couple times before — once when they were teasing these little kids who turned around and, like, beat the living shit out of Thorpe with a barbecue grill, and another time when he made Thorpe fall on some bamboo. The first one was pure luck, he knew, but the second one he'd meant, and he did not like the feeling. Thorpe, it seemed, was about to get hurt again in a big way, and Pembroke did not know how to stop him.

"Is there no one here who would like to put a quarter in the machine so that I can get myself *out* of here? Pembroke, where are you, my boy?"

Pembroke froze by an oversize foam sledgehammer.

"Pembroke, help a friend out, Pembroke. Pembroke?"

"What?"

"Do you suck motherly dick?"

"No."

"Well."

"What?"

"Get over here and drop the quarter in the slot. I will *pay* you back."

"You're going to get all —"

"What?"

"What."

"I'm going to get what? I'm going to get bigger, is what. I'm going to get bigger than this whole building, is what you're afraid of. My arm is going to be like a big log from Superman's planet, and I'm going to make it go through the wall like it was dough. I'm going to have nice big falcon wings, and I'm going to soar over all of you."

Thorpe banged his elbows against the walls of the machine as he narrated his flight from the comedy club, his face pinched and sweaty. Pembroke retreated to the stage, where a door let in from the dressing rooms. The space was big and empty, with mirrors on all sides. Pembroke had in his hands a long mic stand, and he watched himself swing it around the way a ninja would. In the corner there was a man-shaped doll that his father would often beat upon in his performances. Its name was Kevin. That had been his specialty, his trademark — beating the shit out of cloth dummies. He would jump up high and kick the thing in the head so hard that the cloth actually made a snapping sound, like a board breaking. When Kevin fell to the stage floor he would wrestle with it, shouting, "Why are you so big? Why are you bigger than me?" It was the last thing Pembroke remembered seeing his father do.

At the end of the night, Bruce and the Obelisk dragged Thorpe out of the dryer and put him in a wagon because he couldn't feel his legs. Everyone else walked home, because flight pods were for pussies.

Pembroke went upstairs, put on his pajamas, and sat on his bed, holding the unopened box between his knees. Clay was not going to like it, no matter how the issue was presented.

•   •   •

After school, Pembroke designed roller coasters. He had gotten the job by falling in with some amusement park enthusiasts at the cafeteria. They were tired of the same rides again and again. They were not interested in being tossed aloft by these crass, over-wrought machines in the same way that their fathers had, and their fathers before them. They felt that fear was an outmoded response, not worth their time. They wanted a vehicle that would shake them up inside, get them to feel something new. Together they designed a unit called the Diaspora, which took its passengers slowly up a steep incline for twelve hundred feet. At the peak, the coaster stopped and everyone had to get out and climb down a narrow stairwell to the ground. Some steps were deliberately brittle, so that if one person broke through, she could bring the whole group down with her. No one had any idea how popular it would become. Crowds flocked to the ride right from the start, but especially after the first three deaths. Passengers who made it all the way through were fatigued, confused, and disoriented. Some lost the power of speech, or became wildly incontinent. The park management quickly erected an exit tent to handle the serious casualties caused by the ride.

On television, Pembroke took full responsibility for the deaths and other pain caused by the roller coaster. "Look," he said, "I am not an entertainer. But people are clamoring to get on my roller coaster even though they might die. Does this mean people are not afraid to die? I don't know, but it means something. It means that I have built a really effective amusement ride."

"Even though not all of your passengers will make it through alive," observed the host, leaning toward Pembroke.

"I hope more people die on this ride. I hope everyone dies. That is why I built this coaster."

"To kill?"

"Absolutely. Then at least they'd know they really felt something. If you don't want to die, don't come to my roller coaster.

But if you have thought about being killed real high up with no one to help you or lift your dead corpse up out of the ride, you will have a great time."

"You have a dead father, right?"

"What does that have to do with the fact that you're queer?" The host was urged to wrap things up. "What's next?"

"A coaster that's just slightly faster than the swarm of pissed-off bees that will be following its pollen trail."

•   •   •

"I know what you've got in there," Clay said from the hallway.

"I don't see how you could."

Pembroke knelt on the floor of his bedroom and gently lifted the helmet from the molded foam packaging. It had more fur on it than he had expected and was cut in a different style than he'd ordered, not to mention the color, which was beige, though he'd ordered black.

"Pembroke? Come on, man. This is way unfair."

Pembroke adjusted the chin strap and fitted the mouthpiece by biting down hard on the malleable plastic.

Pembroke had received Clay after his real father accidentally set fire to his own face at the Dogwood Days parade. Up until a few years ago, when a real dad died or went away, kids got a robot to take care of them. Clay was kind and patient to Pembroke but did not like him to remember his real father or have any connection to that life. He tried out different names for the boy, hoping, in some way, to erase even this fragile mark of the past. None of them ever took. Pembroke was Pembroke, and that was that.

"Pembroke?" Clay called out again.

"Shut up, you. I'm talking to my dad."

.   .   .

The casts came off, and Thorpe was back to his old ways, except that he had to wear one kidney on the outside, in a little gauze bag. The two of them were out messing around in the streets early in the morning, the sky crowded and gray, flecked with tiny flashing lights.

"I'm getting on that," Thorpe said, jogging toward a fast-food restaurant built in the shape of a chicken.

"Hey, remember that helmet?" Pembroke called out after him.

"What helmet?" Thorpe was balancing on a broken turn-pike divider, trying to grab hold of one of the bird's wings.

"The one that lets you talk to your past?"

"Hey, man, keep it quiet. I told you those things were way uncool." Thorpe's kidney quivered as he struggled to mount the building. Pembroke was sure he could see it throb violently like a water balloon inside the bag.

"Anyway, I'm doing it. I can talk to my dad."

"Can't you talk to your dad right now? Without that thing?"

"That's a robot, dumb-ass."

Thorpe paused, dangling from the bird's crimson wattles. "Shit, dude, you lucked out. That is a cool robot."

.   .   .

The manual said to proceed slowly and carefully when contacting members of the past. "Do not expect immediate results," it said. "Instead, think of your initial three weeks as a 'getting to know you' period. Remember, most of the people you will be contacting will have no idea that such an event is possible. They will not be prepared for their son, daughter, or great-grand-daughter to talk to *them inside their own head*." Most important, the manual said, the user should not attempt to tamper with the past. "Altering the course of history in even the most fleeting or casual manner could instantaneously end your life or the lives of your family."

Pembroke started by talking to his father late at night, just as he was drifting off to sleep. The boy would guess when his father might be on his way to bed and dial in a connection. Sometimes he arrived in the head early, observing in silence as the father brushed, flossed, and examined himself in the bath-room mirror. He was unimpressed with his father's hygiene, noting that, more often than not, in flossing he skipped the back teeth entirely.

When he felt his father drifting off, he would begin to whisper softly, "Daddy, this is your son calling from the future." The voice that answered was deep and powerful, fear-ful of interlopers. But little by little Pembroke, who had ac-cess to all his father's memories, gained the man's trust by predicting specific events that would occur in his future. "You're going to take a drunken swing at your wife tonight and miss, knocking over a ceramic clown bust hanging on the wall," Pembroke would tell him, and the next day his father would answer in dazed and frightened tones, "Son, how did you —"

"Is there anything else you want to know about the future?"

"Will I get married again?"

"Dad."

"Sorry. Will people really fly, and eat a pill that tastes like steak, and wear silver boots?"

"Sort of, but it's so lame."

"I'm going to die, son, aren't I?"

"Everybody dies, Dad."

"But I'm not — I don't want to talk about it."

.   .   .

Pembroke could tell that Clay was pissed. He stopped doing the normal things, like watching the Youth Wrestling semifinals, opting instead to hang out on the miniscule back porch with a fake cigarette.

Pembroke slid back the glass door and joined Clay in leaning over the railing, which let out onto the convenience-store parking lot.

"Clay, what's going on? What are you doing out here?"

"Nothing," the robot answered, squinting as a boy jumped up and down on a wrecked, disemboweled car seat at the other end of the lot.

"Are you sure there's nothing you want to tell me?" Pembroke asked.

"Aw, man."

"Clay, he's my dad."

"So?"

"You don't think that's important? You don't think it would be good for me to talk to him?"

"Dude, he's gone. He burned off his *face*. Meanwhile, I've been here every day, taking care of you —"

"I'm done having this conversation," said Pembroke, and went inside.

•   •   •

Despite the repeated warnings in the instruction manual, Pembroke began, in conversation with his father, to persuade him to do things that would actually change the outcome of his life. First, he stopped his father from participating in the Pepsi-Cola Presents *The Mystery of Mount Saint Helens* float at the Dogwood Days parade. He convinced him that it was better to stay home and watch the event on public access. During a commercial break, though, Pembroke's father saw an advertisement for a three-wheeled all-terrain vehicle, which killed him a year later when he flew off of one and never got up. Frustrated, Pembroke returned to the fateful day of the parade and persuaded his father to avoid the event altogether, perhaps by visiting the free library. He became engrossed, however, in an account of the aboriginal cliff divers of New Zealand, ruining the boy's plans again.

Pembroke worked relentlessly for days, fine-tuning his father's life from the day of the parade until he lived long enough to catch up to Pembroke's own present. It came one morning with little fanfare, no flashing lights or blurry, hallucinogenic images. Suddenly he was just there, really there, living in the house. Pembroke heard him rustling the pages of the *TV Guide* in the living room. He came crashing out of his bedroom and down the hallway to see the old man, whom he only previously remembered as a dim ghost.

"Easy there, Jesse Owens," his father said from the couch, where he was spread out in a pale blue bathrobe, watching a wrestling match.

Pembroke remembered from the instruction book that as far as his father was concerned, life had simply happened to him as naturally as it would to anyone. He had no knowledge of his son's device, only a vague recollection of the distant, late-night conversations. In his father's mind, all of this was completely normal.

"Hey," said Pembroke.

"Hey."

"So. What are you going to do today?" Pembroke did not want to create any disturbance that might, like a sudden wind, make his father vanish.

"I don't know yet. I might go down to the club. Practice my routine."

Pembroke was unsure what to say next. "So you have a job?"

"What? What kind of a thing is that to say to a man in my condition?"

There was a long pause, during which Pembroke's father returned his attention to the match. One of the wrestlers shouted, "Who gave you the nerve to get killed here?"

"Hey, let's go to the midway," Pembroke said.

His father regarded him wearily. "That sounds nice, son. I would like that. Let me get my trunks."

He stood up from the couch slowly, his bathrobe coming undone in the process. Pembroke looked away. His father seldom wore more than a bathrobe around the house, which he left hanging wide open on more than one occasion. Pembroke never had to worry about seeing Clay's pendulous gonads. He didn't think the robot even *had* testicles, and if it did, they would probably look something like a double light switch, or a three-prong adapter, not this knotted, wiry sac plastered to his father's thigh.

They flew to the midway, which was crowded. A roller
coaster loomed in the distance.

"Look," Pembroke's father said, pointing to the looping,
skeletal frame. "It's the twelve years I spent with your mother."
Pembroke cringed at the joke and did not respond. His mother
had died giving birth to him and it was a thing he did not like to
think about.

"That thing's ridiculous. Let's go win something," Pembroke
said, and led his father over to a long row of game booths.

"I'm going to win you something, buddy. I'm going to do it.
An animal, a decorative mirror, that feathery thing hanging
there — you name it."

The objective was to get one of the colored balls in the
clown's mouth. He won on the first try. The barker raised an
eyebrow in surprise.

"Go ahead, buddy, pick out what you want."

Pembroke pointed to a plastic shrunken head.

"You want that?"

"Yeah."

"I mean, that's actually what you want? Out of anything
here?"

"Yes," Pembroke said, unsure what the purpose was of this
line of questioning.

"Oh."

•   •   •

They sat on the boardwalk for a long time, licking sno-cones.
Pembroke's father leaned heavily into his task, slaving away at
the fused mass of bluish ice. For the first time, Pembroke got a

really good look at the man. He was slight, angular, with coarse, coppery skin — it looked as though he'd been made in layers, like pressboard. Other dads strolled by — great, lolling masses of translucent flesh, heaving young children strapped tightly to their chests. They wore pastel shorts and boat shoes without socks. His father looked like someone who might have worked outside, even briefly. He was wearing one of Pembroke's shirts.

"Why do you build those things?" Pembroke's father asked, squinting up at the twin steel loops of the roller-coaster track.

"I don't know. It's sort of like I built them in another life."

"The ones you make are angry, though."

"Yeah, I guess so."

They heard screaming as the linked cars took the first loop. Barely discernible against the sky were the tiny pink arms of the passengers, flailing wildly like the legs of an overturned centipede.

Pembroke's father poured the remaining contents of the cone into his mouth and then, with great delicacy, folded the paper into the shape of a peacock.

"Ever seen one of these?" he asked, setting the bird on the bench seat. Pembroke shrugged.

"When I was a kid, the zoo started giving peacocks away, because they had too many. This was before they started making the animals themselves, when you couldn't just throw them away. Too many had been born, I guess, and they couldn't take care of them anymore. So, for some reason, I decided I had to have one. I carried on for weeks about it until your grandparents finally gave in."

"You had a peacock?"

"No. That's the thing. It died on the way home. It didn't

want to be away from its mommy, or something. Anyway, I remember it lying there in the back of our station wagon, just looking at me with one eye, its feathers spread out, beautiful there."

"That's pretty funny," said Pembroke.

"Yeah," said his father, letting out a breath that seemed to crush his torso.

.   .   .

They were silent for most of the ride home. Pembroke feigned sleep in the backseat, clutching the shrunken head in slick, sweaty palms. The afternoon sun burned a rectangle on his face.

He felt a sickness well up deep inside him, brought on by the presence of his father. He felt terrible about what had become of the old man — he wished he could rub an ointment into his father's life, lay on a warm, medicinal salve that would revive him. The real source of Pembroke's shame, though, lay in the realization that he wished he had not brought his father back at all. Having his father around only made him miss Clay and the life he'd had with the robot. Clay was gone, though — in fact, he had never even existed, ever since Pembroke altered the course of his real father's life. There was no longer any dead father to replace. He remembered the good times he'd had with the robot — lighting fires in the back lot, dropping action figures from the highway overpass, playing Executioners with the neighborhood kids. He puffed up like bread, brimming over with the stupid and irreparable mistake he'd made.

When they got home, Pembroke slipped away to his room and put on the helmet. "Hey, Clay, are you out there?" he whispered under the covers, the thick plume of the helmet tenting the sheets. "Clay, I'm sorry. Clay."

There was no response.

"Clay, I'm sorry for everything I did. I wanted what I shouldn't have wanted. My father — that need to know all about my father — that's all over now. I realized today that you're my father. I forsook you and am now getting what I deserve, but I want to get you back."

All he could hear were wisps of static perforating the flat air.

.   .   .

Pembroke awoke to a distant, rhythmic slapping. Peering out his bedroom window, he saw his father in the parking lot, heaving a basketball in the air and catching it in a gloved hand.

He slipped into a bathrobe and slippers and stepped out onto the porch.

"What are you doing?" he asked.

"I heard you talking to someone in your room."

"Dad, I didn't — how could you hear —"

Pembroke's father kept his eyes on the deep, brimming clouds. "I've seen that thing you have in your room. I read the instructions while you were at school. What's going on?"

Pembroke looked down at his hands. "Nothing."

"Are you trying to talk to dead people?"

"Sort of —"

"Who are you trying to talk to?"

"Well, see, at first — at first, I was talking to you."

"What?" His face collapsed.

"Yeah, well, I sort of — see, you used to be dead, kind of,

except that I talked you out of it — being dead, and now you're alive, but it's like you've never been dead. But the person I was just talking to —"

Pembroke's father crossed his arms, as if in preparation for a cold wind. He shook his head slowly.

"It was an accident. On a parade float. Your face burned off."

His father dribbled the ball with his gloved hand.

"It happened," said Pembroke. "I'm sorry — it all happened."

"I can't think about this anymore," his father said, and sprinted off toward the convenience store. He stayed in the store for a long time. Pembroke could see him through the massive display windows, wandering the aisles in his bathrobe and baseball glove.

Later, he returned, his face smeared with mustard.

"Okay. So let's just say you did — do what you said. Who were you just talking to, then? I heard you talking to someone else last night."

"Oh, that — that was the dad I had when you were dead. He was this robot that got sent to me to protect me when you died. He raised me."

Someone pulled up in the parking lot behind Pembroke's father, and he lurched forward, startled. Pembroke stepped back.

"It's disgraceful. A boy prefers a robot to his own father."

"But I —"

"I bred you, son. Put whatever icing on it you want, you came out of this body."

"You don't understand, Dad." Pembroke crossed his arms defiantly. "I — look, this . . . this robot, in that other life, the one before you came along, he raised me. I can't erase that. I know that we're in this, like, totally *other* different life now, and it's very confusing, but I can't get rid of him in my head. I still have that life in me."

His father shrank back, looking away as if from a health-class filmstrip. "So you brought me back from the dead as some sort of experiment?"

"Sort of."

"And now you're done with the experiment, is that what you're saying?"

"No, Dad. I love you, too. I don't want you to go. I just want both of you. I was thinking I could make it so that Clay comes back and we could all —"

His father looked at him hard, as if he were getting ready to give the boy a big push. "No, son. Hell, no. I don't want any sloppy seconds."

"What?" Pembroke felt himself going red.

"I'm not an afterthought. I'm no sidekick, son."

"But you — you're —"

"This is ridiculous. I don't want any part of this."

Pembroke's insides felt sharp and bloody. He felt, finally, the courage to say what he'd been feeling since the midway. "Well, I suppose you could, just, you know —"

"Leave? Because that is exactly what I'm going to do." But instead of heading off across the parking lot, Pembroke's father came toward him.

"Dad —," Pembroke protested, realizing, as he did so, how empty it felt.

His father looked wrong, climbing the stairs to the porch, and Pembroke noticed for the first time how similar their heads were — ovular, almond-shaped, like bicycle seats.

"But —"

He went into his bedroom and began to pack a suitcase. Pembroke followed at a distance, watching from the door while his father tossed a stack of threadbare shirts into the case. Perhaps, he thought, the old man had sensed all along that the life he'd led there was nothing more than a contrivance, an imposition. Pembroke shut the door to his room and put on the helmet.

•   •   •

"Dude, I'm telling you, you called just in time," said Clay, handing Pembroke a napkin full of chips while taking a theatrical drag off a cardboard cigarette. "I was just about to be turned into a goddamned bedpan."

It was late at night. On the television, protesters were gathering outside Pembroke's newest coaster, Human Chocolate. The newscaster was interviewing a woman who had been stung more than seventy times during the ride. Her face was puffed like a cauliflower, weeping with pus. He looked over at Clay, reclining next to him, tipping back the tattered ottoman with his heel. Everything was more vibrant there, back in the first life. It had been just a few short moments, but already he felt the sickness dissolving in him like an effervescent candy.

Crutches Used as Weapon

One

We are field-testing the new snow. I am waiting at the summit, pressing the binoculars into my eye sockets, training them on the cloud ship in the distance.

"Go ahead," I say into the speech bead. "Let it snow."

I have been waiting to say this. Instead of laughter in the receiver, or even a slow, empty grunt, I hear only static, room noise, the sound of hot drinks being poured out into paper containers.

Sure enough, though, the snow starts to come. Great sheets of it, pouring out of the belly of the cloud like taffy.

"Number F, come in." It is the Minister.

"Yes, Your Royalty . . . ness, Your Highness. Yes, sir."

"What does the machine say, son?"

I take a look at the machine. It is not moving.

"Well, sir, it doesn't appear to be saying anything just yet." The cloud approaches swiftly, laying out a carpet of dense snow about a mile and a half wide. When the snow falls on the trees, some of them break in half.

The Minister does not respond. Instead, I hear the scraping of a stylus on a slate pad.

"Son," the Minister says after a time.

"Yes, sir?"

"How close are you to the snow?"

I do not respond to the Minister, because the snow is already here. The cloud drapes a massive coat of it, about three feet thick, right on top of the machine and then me.

"Son? Son?" I can hear the Minister calling through the speech bead, but I can no longer move my arm to lift the bead to my face.

Two

We lost our daughter in the new mall. Condescendingly overdesigned and implemented, it seemed the last place a person could disappear into. The wide, carpeted aisles and glass panels appeared to us as massive receptacles, built to draw us in and protect us, channeling us along from one store to the next in a carefully forethought pattern. What purpose could those sleek neon balustrades, the swatches of unbelievably bright, primary-color, faux-tribal murals, and forking, multitiered fountains serve but to deflect tragedy and grief? It was incomprehensible that a body could find its way through this halcyon barricade, and yet we managed, somehow, to misplace her, or perhaps it would be more accurate to say that we put her in a place from which it became increasingly difficult for her to return.

I may have let go of her hand hours before we discovered she was gone. It was hard to tell in that place, immersed as we were in the flow of bodies around the center spire, the puffed, flared cylinder of canvas that brought a centrifugal force to the structure. The one thing I remember clearly was the leering orange clown face that topped a public trash barrel, into the gaping mouth of which a thin, gauzy woman had just inserted a foam tray heaped with a family's worth of crumpled tissue paper and crushed drink cups. Our daughter feared clowns, so I was bending down to shield her from the looming bust when I realized she was not there at all, that the weight I'd been interpreting as her body tugging away at my arm had been nothing but two overstuffed plastic bags. I looked up at Karen, who put as much of her fist in her mouth as she could, as if to bite it off might somehow stanch the delirious onset of panic.

We paced the center court in ever widening arcs, peering wildly into the storefront display windows, because, the logic seemed to be, to look in the crevices, the dark, hushed rooms — the most obvious places — would be to cheapen the disappearance, to disrespect it. We took turns shouting her name, hands cupped to our mouths to channel the sound out over the heads of the passing crowds, the word as it broke away from our faces seeming only to rise and disperse flaccidly into the complex, fluorescent web above, bringing *down* the noise level, as if one's voice could sweep a room clean of sound.

We found an Orange Jacket, a beefy, wedge-shaped white woman, who took us into a small, low room.

"Could you describe the child?" she asked, situating herself in a small yellow plastic chair.

I took the first stab. "She was like this," I said, holding my arms out to my sides.

"When she walked, it was like this," Karen said, walking

around in a circle, hunched over slightly, taking small steps on the balls of her feet.

"And when she opens her mouth you always think she's going to spit something up, but words come out instead."

"She hates fruit," Karen added.

The woman looked at us for a long time. Then she tried to sketch a picture of the child using the information we'd given her. When she was done she passed it across the table to us. "Keep in mind, it's not going to be perfect."

But it was perfect, horrifyingly so. I understood, for the first time perhaps, how erroneous the statement "I felt empty" was — what I felt was *full:* I brimmed impossibly with wild, sputtering dread. Karen sat, folded like a paper crane, in the corner. The office was actually called Loss Prevention.

"Don't panic," the woman said. "We haven't even begun a formal search."

"After that, we can start panicking?" Karen asked. The woman did not respond, only wrapped the sketch in burlap and ushered us out into a waiting room.

Two, Part Two

We watched ourselves on the security monitors while men in light blue uniform tops patrolled the dense arteries of the showroom floors, looking for signs. I paced restlessly, purposefully, aware of my body's participation in a larger, more historically significant pacing, convinced that, given the chance, I could lure the child back into our lives, using my body as a probe, a divining rod. As the day failed, predictably, to do anything but insinuate itself into night, though, my will gave way to a sort of frenzied inertia, which crested as guards ushered the last shoppers from the floor with gentle static prods, and bottomed out at about 2:00 A.M. as a dim, flickering fear.

The first thing I dreaded was that my daughter would not return, but in barely perceptible stages I realized that what I was more afraid of was that the child *would* return. I did not want to have to endure the moment of painful, awkward reconciliation when the girl, rescued from the precipice of some sprawling ventilation unit or the cargo hold of a chalk blue van driven by some swarthy, toothless parolee, would run toward us, bruised, bandaged arms outstretched, wholly unaware of how easily and confidently we'd lost her. It would be, for everyone else who witnessed — the families at home, watching the moment replayed in slow motion on a screen behind the slick, rotund visage of a harried anchorwoman — a shameful riot of light and motion that could not be erased. I imagined how the scene would play itself out as seen from the observation camera, through the choppy blue monitors mounted on the opposite wall of the waiting room. Who were we, loping in the periphery of the camera's gaze? We were not parents. We were patrons, members, enthusiasts.

Two, Part Three

At some point during the night I took a magazine to the rest room. It was a women's magazine, the kind with multiple-choice personality tests that determined one's outlook on life by how many points one accrued by responding a certain way. One of the tests had been filled out. I recognized Karen's hooked, cramped penwork in the arithmetic — the way she crossed her sevens, especially, as if someone could mistake a seven for — what? The results of the test were meant to indicate what type of woman the subject was. The last thing I wanted to know was what the test had to say about how little my wife trusted her own perceptions, so I closed the magazine and fitted it, folded in half, in the orifice of the conical tissue dispenser.

The lead article in the magazine: "Crutches Used as Weapon."

At 4:30 they let us out. "Most children are located within seventy-two hours," they told us. Again, we were told not to panic. We trudged numbly through the cavernous green parking garage, motivated only by the desire to anchor ourselves to the house, barricade ourselves from the ugly new life we'd inadvertently created.

In the car Karen said one thing. "Her hand. The way it —" Her lower lip listed and shook, threatening to give way. "I'm already forgetting."

"You don't forget. It's —," I said. I gripped her thigh reassuringly. "It's not a thing you forget."

Three

They dig me out of the snow.

"Jesus," Hot Brian says. "This snow sucks."

"It's terrible," says Penalty. "It's like a white rubber quilt."

"I can't see," I tell them. I've told them before that I couldn't see, which is why they don't respond in any way, but this time I really can't see. Not even tiny pinpricks of light or patches of color.

"Let's get the hell out of here," they say. If we don't get real snow to happen soon, we will all lose our jobs.

"We should never have told those guys we could make snow," Penalty says as they lift me onto the bed of what I can only imagine to be a helicoptruck.

"Yeah, that was really stupid. What were we thinking?" Hot Brian says. I can feel them strapping my body down with nylon cords.

"Next time, chaps," I say into an undefined cube of air directly above my head. One of them, I can't tell which, pats me gently on the head. They are mouthing words to each other, I can tell. Their lips smack noisily, working out the specifics of some plan involving, I am sure, my dismissal from the project. The vehicle lurches. We are in the air, churning upward toward the cloud.

Four

Immediately, and without forethought, I started telling lies about where I'd been on the day we lost our daughter. I was surprised at how easily I could modify my life and how readily my parents, my brother, my coworkers accepted the new person I had become. The more people I lied to, in fact, the further away from that Sunday afternoon and everything I did (and, perhaps more important, what I did *not* do) I became, so that, presumably, one day the whole four years I'd spent as a father might be successfully and completely excised, like raw footage.

This has not happened yet.

Karen stayed in the house, slaughtering whole hours huddled in one position. I'd call her up from the summit every few minutes on my speech bead, to hear what she saw through the bedroom window. "There's a man in a yellow shirt," she'd say, softly, into the pale blue lozenge, as if I were in the room with her. "Oh, he's just now turned the corner."

Four, Part Two

"Bedtime" became a misnomer — it was no longer a point one got to in a day but something grueling one *put in* for, a lengthy trail along which we lumbered, one hand still holding the last light of the previous day while the other reached out for light that had not yet struck.

Five

When I am not out on the summit with the machine, I work on the basement floor of a converted warehouse in the revitalized district, sketching out different kinds of snowflakes. The people who are paying us want the snow to be as real as possible, which means that each snowflake should be different from all the rest, but so far I have not even come close. I keep drawing the same snowflake. My waste bin is filled with sketches of identical snowflakes.

Because of our proximity to the sea, with its erratic tide, the basement often floods, so our desks are balanced carefully on tall stilts. We sway pleasantly as we work, threading our sketches into a wide data cauldron in the center of the room. On the days of flooding, the water laps gently against the cauldron, so that when we close our eyes during naptime, some of us have dreams in which we lie in sand at the edge of a warm, triumphant body of water, resting our heads on a dense patch of ferns.

Ruth sits at the desk directly ahead of me. She is trying to make the snow fall more gingerly. I keep motion sickness at bay by concentrating on the symmetry of her back, how her shoulder blades really do resemble the graceful wings of a butterfly. I never look for too long, though, because when I look for too long she turns and smiles courteously, her stretchy, made-up face bundled in a burgundy kerchief. She smiles the condescending smile of a woman who is aware that someone's eyes have been drawing themselves across her entire body, and this is always the worst thing to have to see.

Six

By springtime, when the solid clouds came and hung their bold, craterous heads over our sector, snapping plastic satellite dishes from the rooftops down our street and breathing hot, sooty panels of wind into every open corridor, Karen and I had already started to make a habit out of steering clear of the house. The rooms cast an alarmingly bright light at all hours, giving us double vision and trembling fits. The hallway leading to the girl's bedroom was especially bright — light seemed to spring from the walls and floor in fiery waves. It was exhausting, even, to sit completely still for long periods. Put another, less fidgety way, the house would not allow us to grieve. We stayed away for as long a period of time as we could manage, loitering in multi-plex theater lobbies, sneaking from film to film like children — anything to put off the inevitable return to the place where we lived.

One night, sitting in the third row for a film we had already been to earlier in the day, Karen said, "You know, the thing I'm most ashamed of is that what I really miss about her are the things that everyone misses. The sound of her feet clapping on the linoleum in the morning — I long for that. I die inside every time I think of it. And I die again just knowing that some-one else in an office building somewhere deep in the city could predict that I would feel that way, years ago, probably before I was born, and make a commercial about it. I feel like someone has already anticipated my life. I want to feel something new. I want my own feelings."

In the sour green light of the trailer advisory, her face appeared translucent, beautiful. I realized the sort of jurisdiction she had over her own emotions, and I felt myself start to sink away from her because of it. My own feelings were as crudely hewn as cave paintings, a child's tentative stab at the human form — what they called a cephalopod. No matter how hard I tried to fudge the numbers, everything came down to a constant preoccupation with the status of my dick.

Seven

It was Karen's idea to start the garden. I felt it dishonest some-how, as if as a result of our failure to guide a small person through even the most rudimentary social acts — walking, for instance — we should be forbidden the responsibility of ushering on any life at all. But Karen was of the mind-set that we should start small and work our way up — that our real mistake was in starting with such an enormous thing when we had never really taken note of the smaller ones.

The plants that grew were not the ones on the packages. We could not recognize any of the wild, colorful flowers that shot up from the harsh dirt we'd tilled with a single stolen, rusted hoe. The flowers were long and wispy — they gave off great clouds of orange pollen, which attracted strange yellow insects we'd never seen before, long-legged creatures with dark, knowing eyes. They gathered on the padded surface of the flowers and drank, making a faint whirring sound.

It was a beautiful garden, but not the one we'd wanted. Not the one we'd envisioned in the store, thumbing through stacks of shiny seed envelopes. Knowing this, we tended the area obsessively and to exhaustion. Then the clouds passed, covering the flowers with dense ash. They looked like gaunt black snowmen. Then they died.

Eight

"I suppose you've been waiting for this." It is the Minister, calling me from his office at the other end of the complex. He wants me to visit him. When I visit him, he will tell me to pack my things into boxes and leave.

"I suppose that is what I have been waiting for," I say, barely paying attention, just skimming the real content of this discussion.

I already know I am off the snow project. I have stopped drawing snowflakes altogether and have been submitting drawings of
my own hand instead. I wrote "hand sandwich" on one I sub-
mitted to the data cauldron. The next day it appeared on my desk
with the word *heh* written in red pen in the margin. I thought
that perhaps they'd gotten the joke.

"Where are you going?" Ruth asks as I descend the ladder
from my desk.

"This is it," I say, trying to sound as small and hurt as possible, even though what I feel is a sort of dull satisfaction.

"No more snowflakes?"

"Never were snowflakes, if you really think about it."

"I'm never going to see you again."

"Nope."

She turns back to her work. Then she turns around again.
"Wait," she says. "I'll walk with you."

We don't go to the office. Instead, I lead her into the net-
work chamber. She holds onto my arm, just above the elbow,
with both trembling, fussy hands.

"I don't remember being in here before," she says.

"Whenever I think of you for long enough," I say, "we tend
to end up in here."

"Oh," she says.

It is dark in the chamber, and humid. Periodic gusts of wind
burst through the corridor where we stand, rustling her long,
wiry hair as if it were a fancy straw hat.

I tell her I do not want to do the thing that we are about
to do.

"Isn't it a little too late for that?" she asks, hoisting a leg up
onto the steel railing. Her heel gets caught in the grating, so that
the whole shoe comes off her foot and tumbles over the edge

into the blackness. "Damn," she says, and then, taking the other one off, "might as well lose them both. No use for a single shoe." We listen to them ricochet off the sides of the deep cavity.

She pulls herself close to me, pressing my face into her neck. She smells like a false human — the way another sort of creature would assume a human smells. Her presence is as brutal and unyielding up close as I've imagined, but there is also something else I haven't anticipated, a tender spot, a bruise she lets me finger and press with my whole body. She is not the kind of person I imagined would allow this sort of discourse. As she clings to me I can feel some of myself going away — as if my body were suddenly nothing more than a decanter and I could pour myself out entirely, spoil someone else's life with my own dank, ruinous indecision.

Afterward, she returns to her desk, barefoot. I start down toward the office of the Minister. My hands are trembling, so much so that I can barely open the door.

Nine

We were at the theater again. The film we were watching was turgid — it shimmied before us like a block of dead flesh, the ruminative characters inside little more than blurred slivers of darkness. A couple sat behind us. The woman said, "I've been getting really good at closing my eyes through the whole movie." Karen did something with her face that might, in another time, have passed for a smile.

They'd often take trips together, Karen and the girl, and in celebration of their return I'd hide a small toy or some candy somewhere in the house. The child would carefully investigate each room, carefully lifting, nudging, drawing back the fabric of the furniture until she found the tiny wrapped package. Later, though, sometimes days later, I'd find her sitting on the floor right near the place where I had hidden the surprise, waiting for something else to show up. I thought it odd then, but there in the theater, studio logo looming on the screen, I realized that the girl was only training herself for a lifetime of disappointment, the way we huddle close to the people we know best, waiting for something of what we first felt for them to make a new appearance.

Ten

The solid clouds have moved on, briefly. Rather, they were carried off, toted at the end of long ropes by the nighttime dirigibles. It may be the way our eyes have adjusted to such things, but it looks very much as though a part of the sky had been removed as well.

I am looking for work, assuming, each morning, that somewhere there is work waiting to be found.

Karen has been learning to play the piano ever since the disappearance. "It's the only thing that will make my fingers quiet enough," she says, filling the room with the soft, hesitant tones of a consummate beginner, the notes engorged with enthusiasm and shame. Over the months, she's gotten quite good.

When I told her about Ruth, she went straight to the piano.

Now Ruth is gone, too, off somewhere in another city, taking on someone else's slippery desperation. Karen and I sit together on the hard piano bench in the afternoon. I have learned the high parts, and she has learned the low parts. Most of the time, what we are playing is only barely discernible as music. When we know what we are doing, though, we smile quietly and briefly at the resultant song, stuffing the expression back down into our chests before it has exposed us for the people we always had a feeling we'd turn out to be.

D own along the river, cars were houses. It was a beautiful thing to see, especially at night, with all the headlights like jewels in the darkness — some cars even had tin chimneys, which glowed red in counterpoint. It was the area I'd grown up in, although it might be more appropriate to say simply that I grew there, as no aspirant motion was possible. I simply took up more and more space with each passing year, until my body had enough.

Some cops were standing by the window of Donna's car, shining their Bucha lights at her. They were looking for someone, a black male who was selling illegal eggs. He'd been seen in this area, they said, driving a car much like the one Donna owned. "That black guy in that car — I don't know even who this black guy was. I ain't out to do that," she said, trembling in the passenger seat, nauseated by the light, her face converging at odd, unpredictable angles, like complex origami. Even without the sickening lights shining on her, Donna had problems. She had lost some of the front of her head in the last war, but could afford to replace only one tooth, and even this the head salesmen messed up when they fit it into her mouth. She had to talk sideways and rest her face a lot, so often that the cops usually left out of frustration and boredom before getting what they wanted. Sometimes she'd have to give her whole head a slight nap after a long sentence.

"What the hell?" one of the officers said.

The lead cop, an Orange Jacket whose head was thick and oily like a brick of meatloaf, leaned in closer to the window. "Could you please repeat what you just said, ma'am. In English, please?" The other officers snickered faintly, cupping their mouths.

"That black type in that car — I do, does not know, still, who was that black type." Donna had a drool cup around her neck, and the drool cup was full. Mr. Sensible tried to tip the cup out onto the road in order to empty it, but when the Orange Jacket saw the skinny hand creep out around Donna's neck from the pitch-black backseat he backed away, brandishing a Very Pistol. The cops also got nervous and put their hands on their holsters.

Wes carefully took hold of my arm. Wes and I were stuck to the wall of The Factories, wearing our giraffe suits, dangling just over the cops' heads. We were supposed to alert Mr. Sensible whenever cops came around. That was half of our job. The other half was bringing illegal eggs around to expecting families. We were supposed to be in stork costumes, but those were hard to come by. Anyway, Mr. Sensible was not going to be happy with our performance.

"What the hell is that hand doing in there, lady?" the Orange Jacket said, backing slowly away, aiming the pistol directly at Sensible.

"I can't barely say."

Mr. Sensible stuck his head out of the window. He was wearing the silver helmet of a Family Getter, and it shone like a mirror ball in the light the police made.

"This woman here," he said. "Why are you bothering her?"

"You should know why. Now get out of the car."

"Listen, you gentlemen are looking for someone black?"

The police nodded.

"A genuine black, no tints, no masks?"

They nodded again.

"You're in the wrong part of the neighborhood, sirs," said Mr. Sensible. "We've sprayed for blacks here. The blacks are at the river, performing a baptism."

The police bought it.

"The police bought it," Wes whispered.

Sensible stuck us to walls, different walls each night, and told us to watch over things, and in return he gave us fish eggs and fish tarts, bags of tiny fish fins. We were thick in the waist from rich fish oil.

The police went down to the river, and everything got quiet. Donna fell asleep, slumped at the open window. Mr. Sensible sat in the backseat, smoking a long, slow-burning cigarette. It started to rain so hard that when the police attacked, we saw only the flash of the guns in the distance. Mr. Sensible put the seat back so Donna could rest. He rolled up the window, rain pelting his shiny helmet as he did so.

The next morning Sensible took us down from the wall, unhooking us with a long metal pole.

"Are you going to kill us?" Wes asked.

"I should kill you," Sensible said, sighing. "I should bury you both alive in hot sand." He handed us each a brick-sized parcel of freeze-dried eel. The scent of the package was so overwhelming that I took a tiny, dime-sized crap in the giraffe suit.

I forgot to mention the worst part of our job, which was to carry Mr. Sensible and Donna around from family to family in a rickshaw he'd found behind the corporate park. He'd fetch the eggs from a distributor or sometimes from his own sources and seal them in the egg basket, and then Wes and I would drag the rickshaw around the neighborhoods until we found the right house. We would show up at the family's door, lugging the unwieldy, temperature-controlled container behind us. The hardest part was that we had to keep the suits on at all times. If we left them somewhere or lost them, or if they were stolen, we would be fired on the spot. Keeping a job here is like clinging to a thread on a rapidly unraveling garment. The more you look at it, the less there is to see. So we always wore the suits. Even during naps.

"Hey, Sensible," Wes said, trudging next to me, draped in shabby, clotted fur. "Weren't those cops looking for you last night?"

"Yes."

"How did you get them to go away?"

"Cops do love to go to baptisms."

Mr. Sensible was Wes's father. They had always been in business together. Before the Child Harvest they sold bolts of fabric to military officials looking to spruce up their uniforms. They were making forty times that money in the egg trade. My own father died in the last war. He wasn't actually in the last war, just close enough to the fighting to get killed. He died while folding a piece of paper into thirds to put in an envelope. It was a letter he wrote to my mother, who was living on the moon platform. He had not seen or heard from her in seven years. I never found out why she left and did not come back. One day she was simply gone, the house still crowded with her rich perfume. "Words fly up" was how his letter to her started and ended. In the middle were a bunch of phrases no one is allowed to use anymore. He hadn't even gotten the letter into the envelope when he was sprayed down with Ending Gel. I know what the letter said because I was the one who sprayed him down. I tore the letter from his gnarled, dead grasp. It was an honest mistake, killing him — he was naked at the time, just lounging around in his car without a stitch of clothing on, the spitting image of an enemy soldier. Maybe it was less of an honest mistake than I am making it out to be, but I don't like to think about it just the same.

Wes is pure black, Mr. Sensible is pure black, but I am something else. A mixture that seems haphazard and desperate, wholly unlike my mother, whose flawless skin was two-toned, like camouflage, each lovely patch a part of the magnificent tonal map of her body. I am just sort of gray. Donna is white, see-through white, like a plastic fork.

We all went down to the river to see if we could gather any eggs from the corpses — Wes and me in front, slogging through the bushes, Donna and Mr. Sensible in the rickshaw.

The only tape we had to listen to on the tape player was one we'd recorded over by accident one night at Sensible's house, which is where I've lived since I was eight. Instead of music there was only the sound of us doing the things we did when we did not know we were being taped, like noisily washing dishes or having an argument about coated cereals or how many legs an ant had. We blasted the thing all the way down the trail to the river, almost blowing out the speakers with the volume on ten, just *trembling* there, taped to the bench seat. Nobody else cared much for the tape, but it has always stirred some unfinished, primal component deep inside me. It sounds remarkably like a family edging its way around a stuffy, indistinguishable evening at home. At one point on the tape, near the end, Sensible yells at me for dropping his lucky spoon. As he shouted he pointed at me with a long, trembling hand, and I swear that on tape you can hear the finger quake violently in the air. To this day, it is the only record I have that anyone ever took more than a passing interest in my development.

First we saw the smoke, still rising from the campfire that had been doused with water, probably by the worshipers right before they died. Then we saw the dead worshipers themselves, all laid out in a circle. Some of them had robes on, white or blue robes, filthy with blood. Their skin was dry and blistered, most likely from the Crazing Rifle that one of the officers was carrying. Everything was all rained on.

Sensible got out of the rickshaw to investigate. He knelt by a woman who had died in a fetal position, hands covering her face. As gently and respectfully as he could, he drew up the woman's robe and unbuttoned her uterine flaps. He fished around in the holes with a gloved hand.

"This place has been picked clean," he said, shaking his head slowly. "Should have known."

A sky tent passed in front of the sun, making everything dark for a minute. The faces of the dead worshipers went sullen, like the ashes of the campfire. We took pictures of the bodies before they got erased. Sometimes a family member would pay for a photo of the deceased to bury when no body was available.

"Next cop I see, I'm'on eat." Mr. Sensible climbed back into the rickshaw. He lifted Donna's slack arm, the one that didn't work, one that she kept around simply to show off that she had been born just the same as us, and wrapped himself in it as if it were a silk scarf.

I thought about eating the cops, which part I'd have to start on. The ass, probably, which had the sweetest meat. Didn't it? Anyway, I would eat the ass and like it. I got real hungry for cop ass.

"Let's get a move on out of this," Mr. Sensible said, waving his free hand out over the dead. "I've got a client at two-thirty."

"It's only nine-fourteen," I said. "What are we supposed to do until then?"

"Good question," said Sensible, rubbing his upper lip with a slender forefinger.

We decided to cut through the park to see the living phone. Some scientists had been displaying it in the square for some time, but then they forgot about it, primarily because the building they worked in got smashed in the war. So the phone was left out in the square, locked in an intricate, bell-shaped iron cage. People fed it when they had food. They'd pass small crumbs of beef or corn bread between the bars. This was not the kind of food the phone was used to, so it never ate everything, but it didn't seem upset when beggars carefully swept up the remains into their waiting food sacks with long whisks.

The phone could not make calls anymore, but it could talk, and if you asked it the right kind of question, it would answer you and was always right. Mostly, though, it just sulked, cowering at the opposite end of the cage.

When we reached the square we cleared the small crowd that

had gathered around the phone by shouting and swinging wooden bats. One man in the retreating group mistook Wes and me for rabbits, muttering something under his breath as we ushered them away. I smashed him in the shoulder with my bat, and it stuck there because of the rusty nail I'd pounded into it a week before. The man fell to the ground like a frail paper kite, taking the club with him. Some friends of his dragged him away. Everyone else cleared out of the square quickly.

"Look at the size of it," Wes said. It was big, about the size of a gorilla. I'd imagined something smaller. Even while I was actually looking at the thing, I was thinking to myself that it should have been a lot smaller than it was.

"Son," said Sensible, "go ahead and ask the phone a question."

Wes looked at his father. "What sort of thing should I ask?"

"Just ask it something you truly want to know. It can tell when you're being sincere and when you're just taking it for a ride. Go ahead — ask it something good."

Wes approached the cage, touching the tarnished bars with his fingertips. "How long until we run into the moon?" Wes asked.

The phone did not respond. It was barely moving at all.

"Okay. Okay. I've got a question," said Mr. Sensible. "If I were a woman and this lady were a woman, and we had a child, what would the gender of that child be?"

The phone only heaved, scooting backward as far as it could go toward the other end of the cage.

"Damn," said Sensible, rubbing his chin. "Donna, baby, stump this motherfucking phone, would you?" But Donna was asleep in his lap. A cold pool of mouth juice was forming on his thigh.

"I don't have anything to ask," I told Sensible, who was looking at me hard.

"Ask the phone a question," he said.

"I told you, Sensible, I don't have any questions."

"Come on, think. What's something you've always wanted to know?"

"I don't want to know anything. I don't ever want to know things. If I put too much into my head, it might stop working."

"Damn, we came all this way?" Sensible was standing up in the rickshaw. Standing was all he had to do to get his point across. Whenever he stood up, it was as if the sky suddenly stopped and exhaled a brief, powerful biscuit of air in the shape of Sensible.

"Fine," I said. "Fine. Phone, please tell me what my mother is doing right now. And why did she go away, and who was in charge when my second mother got picked? Who passed that through? Was that a joke, to have my father fall for the stool sample collection student, the teacher's assistant, no less? Was that done for my benefit? Because I don't specifically remember what that benefit was. And what about my father —"

"Your father?" the phone shouted, suddenly, engorged with wild rage, "your *fucking father?*"

P eople kept having children, and the government kept taking them away. Then the government stopped waiting for the children altogether and began collecting eggs instead, going door-to-door with a slender vinyl hose fixed to a brass bucket. We wanted, more than anything else, to have a child. Not because we didn't think our children would be ashamed of us, no. We knew that they would be ashamed. Like everyone else, though, we believed that whatever it was we might create as a result of the fitful, brief conveyance of our bodies onto each other could help us reclaim the dignity we had lost simply by agreeing to stay in whatever place we found ourselves. People told us not to think about it. Our neighbors, some of whom had made similar attempts, tried distracting us with rich, heavy foods and outdoor games. It was all useless; we saw this desire marked all over our bodies — little black spots in our life where children should have gone.

Aescha was an engineer's assistant at The Factories, her day punctuated at precise intervals by the contraction and expansion of the major bellows. I was a Behavior Pilot — my colleagues and I went up in teams, seeding the clouds with different suggestive gestural medications. To say that the world looked any better from that altitude was an incredible overstatement — the sky was brown and indignant, heavy with Fud, making a mockery of what went on below. It was easy to lose all sense of where you'd come from. Still, though, it was quite something to see, these great planes in formation, cutting a ragged swath in the air. Something close to what one might call uplifting.

From the ground, one witnessed the fruits of our labor as a fine, burgundy mist that spread quickly in broad, tenebrous sheets and evaporated so soon after contact with the earth that it seemed as if it might never have been there at all. Aescha often woke to the tiny droplets tapping at one of the floor-to-ceiling windows along the south wall of our apartment. From the bed she could see the parking lot, where, on a good day, whoever was out there would start to move in perfect unison with everyone else, as if in an elaborately staged dance.

The city we lived in had been recently and brutally reworked to resemble a bustling, late-nineteenth-century industrial center. Old buildings were made to look new, and the new buildings were made to look old. Certain clothing styles from that era returned vengefully and without warning on the bodies of those of us who lived there. We hobbled around in ludicrous, binding pants and topcoats, wielding elaborate, useless canes. I felt the desire to live this way less urgently than most of the people I knew — perhaps because, up in the air, we were relatively immune to the behavior we were administering. We were required to shower in the solution after each sortie, but usually we got away with a brief rinsing. I would go home afterward and find Aescha curled up inside the kitchen cabinets, head in her hands, weeping.

We decided to have a child underneath the amusement park, where we were sure nobody would look. Aescha's body frame, we thought, would hide a child well, at least up until the last months, when we could slip away. I worked during the day while she slept, and when she went to work at sundown I would scurry off to the manhole on the outskirts of the park to fashion a birthplace. There was a ledge and a small alcove at the stem of the slender, ribbed pipe I crawled down, night after night, carrying the essential materials I had collected during the day — sheets, a copper cauldron, twist ties, pillows, a rubber bib, and footies. I was stopped twice on the way there, but in each case the officers were my age or older, too old to qualify as Life Architects and, consequently, not overly concerned with what I was up to.

None of the pilots were sure on any given flight what sort of behavior we were administering, or to whom. Only the commanding officer in each squadron, who carried around a sealed foil packet with the proper instructions, had any idea what we were doing in whatever area it was that we were. The officers were tall, bulky women who were required to adhere to a strict vocabulary, none of which applied, even remotely, to us. This seldom mattered, as they were stiffly unavailable to us in any way, a point driven home by the formfitting wooden girdles they wore over their uniforms. Everybody worked, more or less, in silence — we were given a set of coordinates, and when we reached them the commanding officer would peel back the rip wire on the packet and adjust the machinery to whatever specifications had been ordered. There was a clarity to our missions, an infallible protocol that was, perhaps, the only thing of true beauty in our lives.

Aescha wrote down the days in a book, charting out in red pen a precise ovulatory trajectory. The first month we missed, as well as the second. Summer approached — I knew I would not be able to maintain an erection in the heat. "Please, don't think about it. Don't worry. This . . . this failure — it will give us more time to prepare," she said, but she was old and knew as well as I did that our time was short. Night after night she knelt on the floor, attempting with great and desperate enthusiasm to wring some life into my penis, which only lay on its side, breathing heavily like a beached fish. Days, we wandered aimlessly, exhausted and ashamed. Then I heard someone say in passing that a prosthetic surgeon in the city built genital armatures in exchange for firewood. In the middle of June we discovered that she was pregnant.

Shall I say that we were happy then, as we were, for a short time, dangerously elated by this new and sudden transcendence of our condition? Perhaps, but the dread that we might well have to follow through with the plan that we had, admittedly, thrown together with bits of loose fabric and string followed

so closely on the heels of our happiness as to completely over-
take it.

Royston was once a Life Architect, but then he got too old and
had to leave. He operated the rear hose assembly on our plane.
He was cleaning out the drum when I approached him in the
hangar.

"I'll tell you what I think, but you're not going to want to
hear it," he said, lacing the steel chassis with orange gel.

"That's why I'm asking."

"I think you should do what you want."

"That's not what I wanted to hear."

Royston hoisted the drum into the felt chamber. "The fuck
did I tell you?"

"You can't be a pal and tell me what to do?"

"I'll tell you right out of this room. I'll tell you what to do."
He stood up, unfolding the extraordinary length of his body.
"What I would do? I would do it."

"I don't think you would."

"How long has it been?"

"Weeks. A month. A month and ten days."

"This is too long a time. Think of what's there already —
some part of your face is already taking shape."

"We should get rid of this thing."

"See? See what I said? I'm not in the business of telling
people what to do. What people want, really, is for someone else
to tell them what to do, and I don't do that. I'm in the business
of telling people to keep their chalky, perishable lives away from
wherever I am."

I felt terrible, having derricked the shameful details of my situation on Royston, who, like anyone else, wanted only to be left alone. He put his bib in the plastic barrel and left. I sat as still as I could on the bench until I could no longer tell where it started and I left off.

Aescha started to make things for the child — terribly small outfits with wide, misshapen arms and legs, little suits with club-shaped foot receptacles. She lined these articles up along the floor by the TV, where the dancing carbon light gave a convincing impression of movement. The child, it seemed, was already there in the room, watching us with its keen, box-shaped head.

I saw two officers in the lower decks, sitting close on a bench seat. We had just doused a stretch of farmland, a duty we looked forward to for the spectacular show the birds put on in our wake, gathering in elaborate fractal patterns against the sky. The women were whispering to each other, and crying. The larger one unbuttoned her flight suit at the abdomen, and the other slid a trembling hand underneath, nodding her head gravely as she palmed the pale flesh.

As quietly as I could, I went back to my seat and buckled myself in. Outside, a flock of cardinals hovered in a jagged arc, shadowing with eerie precision the flight of the plane.

Aescha was adopted. Her biological parents, she was told from an early age, had died in a cataclysmic cloud wreck, but she suspected that the story was a lie, that they were out there some-where, waiting anxiously not to be discovered. She often drew pictures of them in a yellow ruled notebook, giving each sketch one-half of her features. In her crude pencilmanship they took on the quality of forensic artists' renderings. She went out of her way to point out that for all she knew, her parents could be living in the next-highest apartment, where what we heard at night, for hours and hours on end, was the sound of a metal pipe being drawn across a sheet of thick glass. In the Plaza of the Honorable Dead she would brush up against some older couple and faint, certain that they were the ones. Her anxiety worked itself over into my life — I quickly grew to hate and fear the elderly, and avoided contact with them whenever possible.

She started to show far earlier than we had anticipated. Three and a half months in, her body began to list and sprout. The condition showed up in her face, under her eyes and around her cheeks — her ankles became thick and unwieldy. We were able to stave off some signs with heavy tape and splints, but each morning there were more. People started looking at her. I packed two identical green bags and we headed out into the night to the amusement park.

It was dark out, the sky punctuated only by the tiny, ovular red lights of nighttime dirigibles. Aescha held my arm at the elbow for stability — her ankles were bruised and raw from the tape. We walked slowly and assuredly, trying to look as incon-spicuous as possible.

Just past the supermarket some children approached in a horse and buggy. There were three of them — two girls and a leggy, preposterously oversexed boy, and they wanted directions to the park.

"The amusement park?" Aescha asked. Her hand began, subtly, to tremble. She was going to give us away before we'd even had a chance.

"Actually, we were going in that direction," I said with a deliberateness that surprised even myself. "If you'd kindly —" Aescha tugged at me imploringly. The children looked us over with mild detachment. One girl nodded to the other, and the boy opened the door.

Inside, Aescha kept her head away from anywhere I might be looking. The two girls examined her body carefully from the opposite bench, whispering and holding hands. Both of them wore elaborate, bone-necked dresses with bountiful skirts. The boy removed a copper cigarette case from his breast pocket, fondling it as he searched for a lighter.

"Do you work at the amusement park?" one of the girls asked.

"I work in the kitchens — I make shapes with batter. My wife is in the chorus — she plays the part of one of the fecal men."

"Is that why she's bleeding?" The tall girl pointed to Aescha's ankles. Blood from the tape wounds had soaked through her pant legs.

For a long, precarious moment I lost my breath. My body was neither excessively hot nor too cold — it achieved a sort of lukewarmness. "She —"

"Yes," Aescha said, her voice wavering. "The costume is very painful."

"They're barefoot," the boy said, his lips clamped dramatically at the service end of a thin cigarette.

"Excuse me?"

"The fecal men — they're barefoot. How else could they slide down the dung mound?"

"The legs are prosthetic. I wear them over my regular legs," she said.

"Rubber mock-ups. They chafe," I added.

The boy said nothing, only swung his patchy head back on the plush leather cushion of the bench seat, exhaling a terrible plume of brass-colored smoke.

We continued on in silence. The two girls played hand games, the rules of which, although unknown to me, appeared rich in heritage and tradition. I put my own hand on Aescha's thigh, an action that was heavily discussed in hushed tones by the girls.

I directed them around the left peninsula of the park, past the towers of the haunted airport terminal. There was a service door between two Dumpsters that looked believable as an employees' entrance. Thanking them, we let ourselves down from the high coach. The girls looked out the windows to see where we'd go. One of them held a silver crescent-shaped speech bead to her ear. I took Aescha's hand. The tender clopping of the horses' hooves faded as we approached the door. I looked back and saw only the dim green brake lights hovering in the darkness. We hid behind the Dumpsters until we were sure they were gone.

"Do you think she was calling —," Aescha whispered.

"Stop," I said.

Helping Aescha down the manhole, I felt the weight of her body, the true weight — I had her by the hips, guiding her down the thin rungs of the stepladder, and I could feel this other body going on inside her, this thing that would, birthed in glaring, nude stupidity, reach out for the world, for whoever in the immediate area gave the sincerest impression that they cared about it. Because what we were making was a person, not a thing. We were responsible — *accountable, even* — for the billion tiny disappointments that would accrete in this person like the rings in Archimedes' tub, culminating in the maturation of another club-faced, knockly genetic impression of our own disastrous shortcomings, so that we could finally say with absolute authority that all of it, right down to the bitter, knotted rind, was our fault.

I lay her down on the wheat mattress and dressed her ankles and calves.

"You know that we don't have to do this," she said, gripping the dingy sheet in a tight bundle.

"Yes, we have to do this. We have to."

"We could have the child now. I bet she would be small enough to keep in our pockets. Think about that. We could carry her around —"

"Stop it, Aescha."

There was a grating sound, and then a flushing sound. I sprinted down the tunnel to see what was happening. A squadron of Orange Jackets had arrived and started dumping gestural medicine down the shaft by the gallon. Two of them were slowly descending the ladder, rung by rung, in inflatable safety suits.

I backed up slowly, crouching against the concavity of the tunnel wall. There was no other way out of the tunnel — the Orange Jackets would confiscate our child, drawing it from Aescha's womb with a fetal horn. And then — what? No one knew what happened to the children, only that they were gone.

I searched around in the silt for a suitable rock, one that was sharp or heavy, or both, one that would successfully end the child's brief, troubled life.

Aescha yelped from across the haystack barricade. The Orange Jackets swung their lights in our direction, scooping out the darkness. I climbed over and saw her kneeling on the ground, palms outstretched, covered in blood. She held a small, naked person in her hands.

"It just came out, I don't know how —," she said, sobbing. I knelt down to examine the child. It was the size of a small kitten. I put out a finger to stroke away a translucent flap of amniotic material. It shook in her palms, flailing delicate limbs, mewling.

The Orange Jackets came closer — we could hear them sloshing heavily through the streambed, borne on awkwardly by the rushing current.

"Aescha," I said, shivering, "please help me know what to do. . . ."

She looked at me carefully, thoroughly, and I saw clearly what we had gotten ourselves into. She rose slowly, still holding the child in her hands, and crossed over to the water.

"This is something they used to do," she said, lowering the child into the stream. It sputtered and kicked as the frigid water rushed over its body. "This is how they saved kings." She let go. The child was drawn under immediately, sucked down by the fierce undertow. As the Orange Jackets made their way over the pathetic barricade we saw its tiny head surface for a moment farther down the way, as if to reassure us that nothing we ever did would go unnoticed.

Years 52—59

Fragment

The census takers rounded the corner onto our block.

"Quick," Darren said. "Shut off the hall light."

I did as I was told. I stood real still in the hallway, breathless, while they passed. I could tell there was a whole group of them through the frosted glass in the door.

Darren had all kinds of blood in him. He was full of the world. His palm alone had come from more places than my whole preposterous excuse for a body. Yet it was him they were after, not me. They wanted everybody back inside their original race. My family had always kept to itself, doggedly turning away anyone half a shade lighter or darker. This was suddenly a profound advantage.

"They gone?" he hissed from the bedroom, where he'd wrapped a towel haphazardly around his waist.

I did not answer. They were still too close.

"Well?" he whispered.

"Stop it. They're not gone enough," I said. My arm was shaking, thumb still resting on the light switch. I hadn't been with another man before, at least not one that had been with me in return. Let alone all the colors he was.

The light stopped in the street. Then it started moving backward, toward the stoop.

What would happen to Darren? I heard that they let people with mixed blood choose one strain they'd like to keep, and a machine would separate out all the rest like sand through a sieve. More often, though, they just got taken away for good. Either way, I would never see Darren again.

"Coast clear?" he whispered down the hall through the half-open door. He held a small mirror at arm's length to try to see what was going on.

The light through the glass started to intensify. I heard careful footsteps on the concrete stairs, the heavy breathing of many men.

"Yeah," I called back to him. "Coast clear."

Stupid Animals

I found a dead bee curled on the kitchen floor, its crisp limbs folded symmetrically over a distended yellow abdomen. I have always felt sorry for the bee, which, I was told as a child, has only one chance in its life to sting. The expression frozen on the dead bee's face seemed to bear this out. Its whole head was powdered with fine, cream-colored pollen, a bright reminder of its final indiscretion. Putting the bee in the wastebasket seemed wrong somehow. Instead, I lay on the floor next to the tiny corpse, resting my temple against the cold linoleum so that I could get a closer look and try to stop trembling for a while.

Other animals are stupid, and shameful. The shark, for instance, which must keep swimming in order to breathe. Or the wild redhead duck. My mother often told me that if a wild redhead duck was wounded by a hunter, it would drown itself rather than be caught. She was trying to teach me a lesson, I think, but it never made any sense to me. I knew that when the moment came, I would allow myself to be caught, no matter how desperately I wanted to die. Whenever I think of the duck swimming madly toward the black lake bottom, though, I have to sit in the large leather head, holding on to my knees with both hands. I do not sit in the head so often these days, for obvious health reasons, but when I think about all the stupid animals I always end up there, keening softly, chewing absently at the brutish latex mouthpiece.

Howard will be home soon, carrying shards of frozen chipped beef. It will be difficult to tell what sort of meal we are having until after we have started putting the food in our mouths. Because we cannot stand surprises, we have begun to eat in fistfuls, if for no other reason than to bury the hunger, to get it *over with*. Utensils have become an unnecessary abstraction.

One night we spoiled ourselves and ordered Chinese food. The fortune cookie I picked said only "Sorry." Later on, he pulled out of me, coughing. I found a piece of another woman caught in his teeth. We both examined it, sitting cross-legged on the bed, naked to our socks, the harsh yellow light of the bathroom cutting a distorted parallelogram across our bodies. What I thought of to say was "Do you want this back?" Howard stood up, his hefty form sagging, changing shape as it moved to the door. I heard him shuffling the pages of a magazine in the bathroom. I fell asleep to the sound. I *did* sleep, because this is not a story about how animals are actually smarter than us. Some are smarter, and some are stupid. If I had my choice, I would be something vibrant, spectacular, way at the top of the food chain. I want fangs, elaborate feathers, wild bursts of colorful skin.

I put the bee out on the stoop. Its friend came and circled it.

I have a red car. Whenever anyone asks what kind it is, I draw a blank. I think of all the car names I have ever known, and repeat them one by one until the person is satisfied. I have never remembered cars, only the things that went on inside them. I remember Howard's car, parked underneath a bridge, in a place where it was not supposed to be.

The bee's friend began to nibble at the carcass, or maybe it was grieving. I went and had a cigarette by the air conditioner. The apartment was quiet all of the time that I was there.

Gawain went down in a heap by the stream. I had hit him with a knotted club right in the kidney, where there was less armor. "What kind of a person takes a nasty swipe like that?" I thought, looking down at the quivering hump of his back. I could see that he wasn't breathing right. He sort of whistled through his nose, smacking his lips wildly as if the air were something to be eaten, not breathed.

"Sir Gawain, Sir Gawain?" I said, touching his white cheek with a gloved hand. I was determined not to have this on my conscience. He sighed, rolling his eyes all around, taking what looked like a final survey of his life.

We were alone in the woods, out past the wire fences and the steel observation towers, past the outermost management facility. Instead of the steady hum of hidden recording devices, all we could hear was the distant bleating of strange, terrifying wildlife. We were in the place we had been instructed, during the training period and in our carefully managed nocturnal visualization workshops, not to go. The trees out in this particular zone cast murky, oppressive shadows over everything. Somewhere, in an elevated laboratory, the Life Architects were suiting up, gathering their retrieval instruments to return us to the facility grounds.

Everyone in Subject Group 11 had made an individualized suit of armor. Mine was in the shape of a badger, for sheer strength and connection to the earth. It is a stealthy, hideous creature, banished to the dark woods. The helmet was unnecessarily ornate — I made it by pressure-soaking fat swatches of burlap. The others, dandies all, got theirs made for them in The Factories. I chose the higher road, learning the craft of armor design in the forest, testing different materials for their durability and longevity until I found just the right combination.

Gawain's suit, the spotted owl, a flimsy, degrading garment made from the most insubstantial materials, flagrantly betrayed his youth. Maybe this was why I gave him such an inordinate beating. Or maybe it was the woman he'd left behind forever in order to be here, what a terrible waste he'd already made of his own life as a result. I had lost track of time, chasing him along one of the more obscure paths, a shifty, overgrown trail punctuated by bright orange warning signs. I could not remember the cause of the chase. It was possible that I began chasing him out of boredom or because we had run out of beef. I did not expect to swing at him as forcefully as I did. It was hard to imagine myself as someone who was capable of such a swing. But there he was, twitching, bleeding heavily into the dank streambed.

I thought of the good life we'd been issued by the scientists at the University of Life Architecture: the soothing Styrofoam huts we lived in, the entertainment programs that they streamed in to our handheld data organizers after naptime, the indestructible plastic beverage coolers we had been issued — fully stocked — and how it would be a long time before I could have a proper drink.

"Who goes there?" Gawain swung his arm up above his head. He looked like a beached deep-sea animal clinging to a mossy outcropping of rock. His eyes were wide and dark.

"It is I, the Black Knight. Prepare yourself for the next life."

"Black bastard. Stinking black bastard. Jesus, you've slain me."

"Die with dignity, or you will die alone."

He lapped desperately at the air, sucking erratic mouthfuls.

"You have betrayed me. You have betrayed your friend of all these years." He looked away into the mud, gurgling. There was a lot of blood coming out of his suit. The books the woman at the Conflict Management Facility gave us said that the old knights would bash one another in the armor, crushing their opponents from the inside out, and this was, more or less, what I had done to Gawain.

Before, in the old life, we were programmers at Corporation Two. We worked at a long wooden table, shuttling numbered pucks back and forth between us in accordance with the commands shouted through a bullhorn by our coxswain, Colonel Megan. When we successfully completed a sequence, Colonel Megan would pull a nylon cord and a sugar marble would drop down through the elastic tubes attached to the ceiling and onto our waiting, quivering tongues. If we were good, we got three marbles a day, but we were seldom good. Mostly, we were simply making do, congratulating ourselves if we managed to receive even one marble. It was a life we'd resigned ourselves to, until one morning when I noticed a sign in the fluorescent departmental cafeteria. "Are you a man, ages 21–46, who has ever thought of ending yourself?" it said. Below was a telephone number. I gingerly tore down the sign and brought it back to the lunch shelf where the other members of my division were gathered.

"What is this?" I asked. They leaned in close.

"I've heard about this," Galthon said. "They take you to a secret place and watch you. All you have to do is live. Just survive out in the woods or in the desert for a long time."

"How long?"

"I'm pretty sure it's forever."

"Who are 'they'?" I whispered, aware, suddenly, of how quiet the room had become.

"I think it is some sort of regional branch of the Life Architecture school. I think they just want to see what the world would be like without men in it. To see, you know, if it would make things any easier."

This was enough of what we'd been looking for. Within a few days, we'd all called the number. The operators were cordial, reassuring. They asked for our addresses and told us to wait outside our housing complexes the next morning. They told us to leave as much as we could behind. They told us we'd be going in stages — first for a week, then two weeks, then a month, and then for good, if we wanted. We woke up early the next day, applied our daily food patches, and waited, bags lightly packed. They pulled up in a sleek white bus and drove us out to a shining metal bunker buried in a forest. I just barely managed to leave a note for my wife, clouded with misspellings, cross-outs, and erasures. I could hardly read it myself.

The first week we watched filmstrips in a wide, resonant hall. The filmstrips were all about boys' lives — boys riding skateboards, playing ball games, diving into quarries. The voice-over was in a language we did not understand, possibly Korean, but between the images of the boys there were phrases in black text against a plain white background, phrases like "Which is faster, a train?" We were given ruled pads on which to take notes. In the upper right margin there was a small logo depicting a campfire and the words REGIONAL ORGANIZATION FOR THE END OF MEN. We doodled on the pads. When we were done doodling, the pads were taken away from us and stored in a large, oblong humidor at the back of the room. Then we were separated, issued clothes and rations, and put outside.

Life in the woods, though peaceful, was unbearably dull. We sat for long periods in our paper dungarees and paper hats, asking one another what time it was. No one knew what time it was — that was the joke. Or one of us would put his hand down his pants, unzip the fly, and stick a finger through the hole, claiming that this was his penis. Then it was two fingers, then the whole hand — finally the whole contrivance of the pants was abandoned and we simply showed one another our arms whenever we thought we could get a laugh. We made grass wigs until we were sick of them, and then we made shale puppets until those, too, grew tiresome. One of the older men smeared himself with thick mud and chased us. We slept when the bugs slept.

After a few days, a group of women in white jumpsuits drove up to our campsite in a van and took us to a metal hut at the bottom of a ravine. On the way, they served us long bars of taffy. In the hut they had us sit in a circle and, one by one, tell them what we'd learned. We told them the forest sucked. They nodded and wrote things on a plastic pad. Even the sound of the stylus scratching the hard plastic was a welcome relief from the

hysterical silence of the woods; it was the sound of human inge-
nuity, of survival.

Late one afternoon after the bus had dropped us off at our
campsite, we got drunk on the rationed allergy medicine and
began knighting one another. I don't know where the idea came
from. It just suddenly felt like the only thing left in the world we
hadn't yet done. By the delirious light of the fire we got down
on bended knee, reciting what we could remember from some
of the older fairy tales. We began as the Knight Wrestlers, until
it was discovered that both Gawain and the Yellow Knight had
been trained in the Greco-Roman style. The idea was to start
out with an even playing field.

After that we began fashioning traps for one another, pitfalls
and swinging wooden spikes. Someone dug a pit, for instance,
and nearly everyone fell in. This was better than anything else
we had come up with. This was the salve we'd been flailing
about for desperately. The thin, silent man with the handlebar
mustache, the one who would soon become known as the
Green Knight, delighted us by fashioning magnificent swords
and trick landscapes.

My wife greeted me in the kitchen with the usual projection of
detached irony, clutching her cigarette like a German.

"The old rules no longer apply," I said, toweling off with a
rag. I had been gone for three weeks, earning my first achieve-
ment badge. She only nodded, paging through a meat catalog.
"You want me to become a knight, don't you? You'd like that," I
said.

"I like knights," she said.

"You're looking at a knight. What does that feel like?"

She said nothing, folded the catalog in thirds, and slipped it into the slotted napkin holder. Her hands were trembling. "It makes me feel tired," she said, and went into the bathroom, where she turned on the water full blast.

After that, she spoke mostly in fragments. We started using signs, thumbnail sketches posted to the door. A duckbill, a happy face, double middle fingers. We saw each other fleetingly, extras in each other's lives. I continued amassing the necessary tools with which to perfect my armor.

We were ready for the monthlong stay. The women in the jumpsuits took us into the woods in the sleek white bus and left us there. Occasionally we caught glimpses of them through the trees, writing on their hard pads. We started spending all of our time honing our skills. The Green Knight had been through the service, and was far ahead of anybody. We chose him as our instructor.

"This is what you call your engineer's knot," he'd say, suspended from a high tree branch. We learned the essentials of hand-to-hand combat. It was all about turning our aggression into a fine-pointed stone and pressing it into the skin of our hearts, he said. We held hands in a ring while two of the men beat each other with sticks. "No one leaves this ring," the Green Knight would say, "until I see death's passion show its face in your eyes."

It is true I have made some decisions in my life that were less than palatable, but I do not count my sporadic relationship with Gawain's fiancée among my transgressions. Chelsea was innocent, a girl really, and in serious need of guidance. I liked the way she asked all the important questions right off the bat. We spent hours alone on an orange couch, sharing cigarettes while she enumerated his faults. "We'll be shopping," she'd say, "and he'll start dancing. 'We're lovers,' he'll say. 'What lovers do is put beans in the box. Putting beans in the box.' All this while he's filling the shopping cart. What an asshole."

I felt the end of day coming. Gawain lay still for the most part, give or take a tremor here and there. There was no sign of the others. They had their own battles to contend with, I suppose.

"Are you going to leave me here to die?" Gawain asked, clenching his teeth.

"I have something to say to you, and then I'll kill you."

"Well," he said, "let's get on with it. The pain here is killing me."

I sat down on a nearby felled tree. Darkness crowded up around us in degrees. An animal flashed its green reflective eyes in the distance. I felt the weight of this man's death on my hands.

"Do you think there's any way to bring you back?" I asked.

"A knight doesn't ask for his life back. Death, to a knight, is like peeling back the skin of a banana."

"What kind of pain are you in?"

"I feel it mostly in the extremities. It's like wasps converging."

"I've taken advantage of your betrothed."

Gawain only lay there, mud caking on his face like a primitive mask.

"I have to tell you that I don't think she's particularly fond of you."

"She's not particularly fond of anybody, Black Knight, not even you, though in your heart you may believe it to be so. She doesn't love. Although I wouldn't take it personally, I would not suggest becoming too wrapped up in anything."

I sat there for some time. "The dead play tricks," I said to myself, preparing to brandish my club. "The dead play tricks." Gawain heaved away, his features warped and desiccated.

I followed the instructions my wife had left on the kitchen counter. She was waiting for me at the beach, where the light-house used to be. Long ago, when we were still trying our lives on for size, I would take her there and we would spend all night in the deep cavity the demolition team left when the lighthouse came down, getting out of our heads on pills and brandy.

I sat down next to her on the concrete foundation, handing over a bottle. "You're a good knight," she said. The sea roiled down below, shrieking as it crashed against the jagged white cliff face. It was getting dark — the kind of darkness that crowds over the ocean, where it looks as though the light of the world might suddenly fall down and die.

"You don't frighten me with your tactics," I said. In the distance two kids teased a horseshoe crab with sticks.

She took a drink, slipping her free hand into a pocket. "My only request, in all of this, is that you stop it with the magazine articles." Sometimes I would see something that might be of interest to her, something helpful or affirming, which I would clip out and stick to her car door. The last one was called "She Listened with Her Legs."

"Oh, that will stop all right. You can bet that will stop. You don't even know who I am, do you?"

She looked out at the ocean, where a seagull hung noisily in the ugly purple sky, the unwitting backdrop for our increasingly stupid and irrelevant lives.

"This is an easy thing, if you are using the right colors. Use the right colors, Derrick. You don't have to go away forever. *Want* to be a better person. You make everyone around you sick to their stomach. People hate you. Most of the time, this counts as enough of a sign. But it doesn't mean you have to end yourself."

I took this as my turn not to say anything.

"Ugh. You're the movie someone would watch because the one they really wanted to see was sold out. You're going straight to video, Derrick."

I was all bent up inside, but even so, only part of me wanted to leave, only part was sick and tired of this relentless onslaught. Instead, I sat and watched her go at me like a trained dog gnawing at a policeman's padded arm.

"What about honor? What about faith?" I asked.

She looked surprised, aggressively so, knowing that surprise was the last response I was looking for to such ludicrous, inflammatory questions. Her lips were blue; they trembled slightly in the dim, unfashionable light. "No man is a victim who doesn't think himself one, whether he is king, knight, or knave," she said, staggering to her feet. She handed me the bottle. "Take the house. Have the house. The house is yours to keep." Then she was off along the path, a white blur flagging in the night.

"House? I have no use for that. House? I need no house!"

"Black Knight, Black Knight, please do me the favor." Gawain was getting blue around the eyes.

"Be still. I haven't told you yet the thing I had promised." We heard the whirring of motors in the distance, the deep clang of armored surveillance robots maneuvering through the woods. The robots would find us and take us back to the laboratory, where we would be hosed down and sent back to the corporation, ignominious fools.

"Why do you suppose they'd want to end us?" I asked.

"What?"

"The End of Men. It just came to me — that's what they call this camp. The End of Men. What are they trying to achieve? How will anything, like, *happen* anymore without men?"

"Please, kill me."

I put my hand to my chin, surprised to touch instead the rough, impenetrable helmet I was wearing. It felt funny, unnecessarily so. "Do you think — could life really be better here once we're gone? And how will we know? We won't know. We won't even be around to see how much better things are once we're not around."

"Please don't tell me this is what you've been waiting to tell me," Gawain sputtered, his mouth full of blood. With each word it came bubbling up, staining his teeth a deep red-brown before draining out down his cheeks.

"No."

"Well? Quickly then, quickly."

"Gawain," I said, shifting my weight toward him, "one night, while you were asleep with Chelsea, I climbed in through the window and slipped under the covers right beside her, just to feel her life boiling away. While you lolled heavily in the far corner of the bed I fit my hands into the crescent groove of her clavicles, where her body was most real. 'Take my life, please,' I whispered, pressing my face to hers. Some transfer occurred then, I am sure of it. I got some of myself out — I exhausted myself into her skin. She started to get hot, whereas I was shivering there under the covers. There was a mole by her ear, and by morning it resembled my face."

For what felt like a good minute he made no noise at all. "She does not love, Black Knight. However you felt. It's a load of crap, the whole thing."

"That's no way for a knight to talk, Gawain."

"Oh, get it over with. Can't you see I'm in complete misery?"

I raised the club high into the air. Lancelot appeared at the crest of a hill in the distance with the Green Knight. Red lights from the transmission towers flickered in the heavy evening air; smoke unfurled from the stacks of The Factories. For a moment, all of us were completely still. The night was tacky, sticking to us like old tape.

"In the name of Saint Paul, I hereby condemn you to death." I brought the club whooshing down on Gawain's chest. A sound came from inside, small and hollow like the metal ball in a can of spray paint. In Gawain's last heaving breath, a high, warbling chortle, he declared, "O, I am slain."

Lancelot and the Green Knight approached silently, wordlessly. I had had enough of words at that point. They were something you couldn't get off your body, no matter the amount of scrubbing. Together we lifted Gawain, carrying him to a clearing, where we built up a makeshift funeral pyre.

"Anybody got a match?" I looked at the scared faces of the others. None of us had ever been this close to death, not even the Green Knight, who had only flown over the endless deserts of the Eastern Properties in an officer's skiff. Tears rolled valiantly down Lancelot's cheeks. In the moonlight he looked like a walking woodcut. There was the impulse to say a prayer, but we were at a disadvantage, all of us having been brought up in different faiths. Silence began to feel more appropriate as we went along, so we knelt around the pyre, removing our wildly ill-fitting helmets. "Such a thing, such a thing," whispered the Green Knight, bowing. The lights on the observation towers changed color — a soothing woman's voice issued from the mounted megaphones, beckoning us back to the Styrofoam huts. For the first time in my life, I didn't know where I was going to be the next day. Lancelot struck a match, and soon the whole night caved in around us, swallowed by the towering flames.

T hank you for your interest in applying for the _____ position in Gate 4 of Chamber Complex D. All of our prospective employees are given a rigorous series of tests, from which we decide a candidate's ability to perform in a high-stress, high-sound environment. The Factories are a difficult, often hazardous place to work. It is necessary, sometimes, to maintain a degree of concentration that exceeds the expectations of "the normal." Below is a list of problems and complaints that people sometimes have. Read each one carefully, and in the space below describe HOW MUCH DISCOMFORT THAT PROBLEM HAS CAUSED YOU DURING THE PAST _____, INCLUDING TODAY. Do not skip any items, and print clearly and legibly. If you change your mind, erase your first answer completely. Read the example below before beginning, and if you have any questions, please ask the technician.

Example: HOW MUCH WERE YOU DISTRESSED BY

Q: *Body aches?*
A: Often, particularly after gardening.

Headaches?

Sometimes I can feel the inside of my head, right along the temples. Certain objects resonate there — a metal fork, for instance, makes a sound that is like a squealing tire. I played with marbles as a child, and one of them was clear and lit from the inside with crimson and yellow. Had I not lost it in a gutter outside of Golf City when I was eleven, I would have for you a perfect visual representation of this phenomenon. You might claim it was better this way. I, for one, do not take the loss of possessions lightly.

Feeling lonely?

Before I lost my wife I had only ever hit one other person, and that was in junior high. His face is like a cotton swab in my memory now — he floats there in slow motion, holding a black book bag over his groin outside the locker room. It's the Sesquicentennial and we're getting out early to see the tall robots. I remember the scent of a person, the way it changes the air in a room. Louis Burney smelled like hair and lighter fluid — he came from the developments, where kids pissed out their territory and traveled in herds. I hit him in the gut — the reason isn't so important anymore. The sound, though, is the thing. Like two sounds at once — and one of them is like the whole world just lifting up and folding over.

Feeling fearful?

When I tell people that my wife and I terminated our relationship, what I really mean is that one day I came home from work and she was gone. It was not so much the things she took with her that made me fearful, but what she left behind: two sweaters, yellow and brown (which I had given her — coincidence?), the remote control for a VCR that she took, a set of fine German knives, subscription bills for *Solder & Wire* and *Bulletin of the People of the Living Phone* magazines, three large plants whose lives I am now wholly responsible for, and a journal, blank but for the upper right margin of each even page, where the phrase "had fun" is marked in her telltale cursive. When I knew she wasn't coming back I gathered the items in the living room. Humped there on the floor, they seemed to twitch and breathe, like real animals. I slept for two and a half days.

Having ideas or beliefs that others do not share?
Breathing into a plastic bag changes the humidity in a room. A carpet knife can be useful in the removal of ingrown toenails. Not all bad people are French, but all French people are bad. Select meats, when buried for six months or longer in fertile soil, can be used as a medicinal poultice. My brother's arms are kept in a jar at the county medical examiner's office downtown. Two nails in a board will weaken its integrity, but not three or seven. The earth is bulging over Canada. When the light hit him just right, my father looked like an outboard motor — pull the cord and off he'd go. People's breath is almost always more important than what they say. Lifting weights will get you nowhere. When rain falls, something else is always going up. Shoes are for the weak.

Blaming yourself for things?
There were holes in our basement walls where the enemy soldiers were shot during War H. We dug around the foundation of the house, but our search for their remains was fruitless. We had

more luck with the arrowheads. Scott earned a merit badge with his collection. The rest of us couldn't make it further than Tenderfoot. I learned to masturbate in a tent with two other boys and when I came, the lights went out. I saw visions — what I thought then to be the devil's palm pressing my face into the sleeping bag. The other two had done it before, and only nodded when I recounted what had happened. Later my dick grew to twice its normal size. I panicked but the others reassured me. "Rest it up awhile," they said, kneeling by the fire.

Hearing voices that other people do not hear?
My mother would break things — I heard it through the wall. Later in life, the same sound would crop up unexpectedly — at an important business meeting, say. Once I heard a whole flotilla of saucers hit the floor while boarding a bus for New Livonia. As for voices, I can't say for sure, especially on condition that they're not mine. Part of me talks in another language, which is like having an itch you can't scratch, or when you're holding a screaming child. I'd hit the kid, which is why my tubes are tied. You won't see any more of me once I've left this earth. That's one thing I've always had a corner on, so to speak.

Repeated unpleasant thoughts that won't leave your mind?
I play the trumpet, and I do most of my unpleasant thinking when I am practicing. If the image of someone smashing my face into the curb, teeth first, rushes into my mind while I'm playing, for instance, my lips will tend to purse instantly. Other things I think about are the sound of two hollow metal tubes colliding end on end, catching a nail with my eyelid, silverware that has not been cleaned, how much a snakebite would hurt, climbing somewhere and not being able to get down, getting a

paper cut on my eyeball, the lottery, having my knees bent the wrong way, swimming headlong into the propeller blades of a ship, having my teeth sanded down to sharp points, genital self-examinations, competitive sports, who will be wearing my organs when I die, and the fear that I am slowly bleeding to death from the inside.

Having to repeat the same actions, such as touching, counting, washing? When I touch things, I can hear them break. I can hear the sound they will make in the future. I touch lots of things. When I touch a person I can know her faults. If I'm touching someone on the top of the head, I know exactly where his weak points are. The same is true for animals. My neighbor, in the life I used to fool people with, had an Irish setter named Pippin. "Here, Pip, come on, boy," he would say to the dog from his porch door. I held the dog's snout in my hands, and it told me about all of my neighbor's secrets because it hated him. He was a wife swapper, which explained all the nice cars in the driveway. "You're a good boy," I would say to the dog, slapping its hindquarters, "you're a good old boy."

The idea that you should be punished for your sins?
My father owned a horse farm and drove trucks and cars into the quarry for extra cash or food. We could see them sometimes from the rope swing — bruised forms sulking at the bottom.

I pulled my first pair of pants down near that same quarry. It was late evening; Dad nearly ran us down on his way to the water's edge. We were hiding in the tall grass. My dick made a sucking sound, like a bad drain. Her name was Pam — she started to cry in the darkness.

Later that summer we attended an outdoor piano concert.

We didn't think to bring a blanket, so we sat on the grass. The piano was like a thousand knives hitting me in the chest, one after the other. I would not see Pam again. She is pregnant now, living somewhere in one of those big boxlike states. I burned all of my pictures of her, something I've come to regret more than almost anything else, after all this time.

Feeling afraid you will faint in public?
In grade school we had an assembly. A man came to talk to us about the dangers of smoking. He had a hole in his throat and spoke with the assistance of a small machine. The room was dark; we were shown slides of the operation. One shot showed a nurse slipping her finger into the hole, right down to her knuckle. I started to see colors. Everything was far off, all of a sudden. I made my way to the back of the auditorium, where I collapsed, vomiting my lunch by the ticket booth. A guidance counselor found me there and admonished me for trying to duck out. "I'm sick," I told him, wiping my face on my sleeve. "Nice try," he said, dragging me back to my seat. "Nice try." I thought this event would follow me for the rest of my life, but soon enough everyone was already on to the next thing.

The idea that someone else can control your thoughts?
We made sure our linens were dull and muted in color. Gray on maroon, navy on black, brown on black. My wife was concerned that bright colors would hurt the house. She drew the shades whenever there was a thunderstorm because the lightning put streaks in the linoleum. She had a thing about light — she wore tinted glasses in the house, which made her look like someone from another time. It made her teeth look like big

planks. She was like somebody's understudy in those glasses. When we fought I would make a bonfire in the backyard because I knew she would not follow me there. I could see her watching me through the attic window, sucking on an inhaler. I'd throw another log on the fire, sending a volley of sparks high into the air. This nearly always made her disappear for a few hours. Sometimes it rained. This, to her, meant victory.

Other people being aware of your private thoughts?
I didn't like the way my life felt on me. Cumbersome as an old jacket. I visited dark places, bars with an entrance at both ends. I never used that back door that I can remember, but its presence there was essential. Somebody was always throwing darts. "Jesus," I would think to myself, "those things are coming right for me." One night a man in a green parka came in. He walked on thin, moon-shaped legs and sat in the chair next to mine. He was looking for clues as to the whereabouts of his son, who had crashed his motorcycle right outside nearly three years before. I told him I was a relative stranger, and he held out a photograph. It was his son. They both had the same long face, like the wooden handle of a gun. The police had dismissed the case, he said. His son did not commit suicide, no way. I excused myself. There was too much life hanging around him. I could feel his heavy breath. In the lavatory sink my hands grimaced, slick with liquid soap.

Loss of sexual interest or pleasure?
Not hardly ever.

I woke up in the back of a stranger's car, a vast blue sedan with cigarette burns on the dash. Hard to tell what hour it was from my vantage point on the floor, the pale green light held high above the city in the distance as if by a teasing older brother. My neck was all bent and crooked, a hard impression of some car part pressed into the back of it. My whole body was caved in and folded like the thousand facets of a crushed aluminum can. I needed the pills. Nothing any doctor had done could come close: the weight treatment had not worked, neither had the saline injections, medicinal salves, the gyroscope, the boulder toss, submersion in the warm chemical baths. But those pills — not a whole lot I wouldn't do for those pills, tiny plastic jackets of blue and white, the fine yellow substance inside that glowed like a burning star under black light. Pills that made you feel like an angry, hideous young bull let loose into the fighting ring. Susan would fix me up with a bag, I was sure of it.

I sat up. I had somehow gotten myself all the way out to the bay, which reflected a brilliant array of colored lights that hid its true, rust-colored ugliness. The couple I had followed around the night before had left no traces of ever having been here. Yet there was a conversation that I was sure I could remember snippets of — the woman talking about a doll's head she used to comb in her backyard, how dirty the spring is with everything smelling like cold semen in the air, and what made a billfold different from a wallet. We met at a nightclub, one I'd come to in search of a hit. I used to go there a lot to pick up different things, but the neighborhood had changed since the last time I'd been there. It had whitened. So instead of the pills, or anything I could really make use of, there were these people. We started talking about sex — the woman told me I was being too uptight. I didn't even know who she was. I got up to leave, but she took my arm and yanked me back into the booth we were occupying. Her face was nested in the center of a mess of matted, crimped brown hair, floating like a shrunken head. I remember telling her to stay away from my life. I remember that we all decided to take a walk.

.   .   .

Susan was my old girlfriend, and she lived somewhere nearby. It had been a long time since I'd seen her. She was all sorts of different races — shades of black, with splashes of white and something else — the kind of shit no one could get away with anymore. Thirty years ago this kind of breeding was fine — encouraged, even. It had been completely legal to "mix and match" before the Voiding Initiative. She passed, though, fooling the Orange Jackets until the property-wide blood census. That was pretty much the end of our relationship. I am as white as a household appliance, and I was not going to jail over this woman.

•   •   •

My clothes sat heavily on me, bent with sleep. There was a metal kiosk in the distance, shaped like a paper milk carton, with someone official-looking inside, all dressed in orange. I thought I saw him look at me and then go for a phone. Feeling around for my belongings, I picked up a crushed straw cowboy hat — something stupid the woman had put on my head at the nightclub. The man had laughed. "He looks just like that fellow ———." His inflated grin was too much for me to handle. I only wanted to wear the hat more, placing it on my head like a true rancher.

There was nothing else in the backseat but an empty water bottle and some magazines, so I slid out the door that was farthest away from the guard and crawled over to a set of high green Dumpsters. I heard a voice — "Hey, this is a — Hey, goddamnit, this place is —" It was as halfhearted an attempt as I'd ever heard. From behind the Dumpster I could see him standing outside the kiosk, hand held like a visor against his forehead to block out the powerful floodlights shining from the roof. He looked at his watch, pacing the length of the concrete loading dock. Two truancy robots flew by overhead, ripping open the night with great big searchlights. I was going to have to make it through another day.

As quietly as I could, I hopped the fence and set off on a dirt trail that led through a construction site. Giant, wiry structures, like the bones of a primitive monster, rose up on either side of me, black against the loud green cityscape. There were rows and rows of cranes and backhoes, their sharp, slender appendages hanging desultorily. I might as well have been on another planet.

.   .   .

I hadn't seen Susan in three years, but I was sure she could hook me up — she always seemed to be surrounded by people in the pharmaceutical business. "I see absolutely no reason why I shouldn't just go on taking these pills for the rest of my life," she had said one night, breaking the long silence we often observed after coupling. "You're crazy, you actually . . . ," I said. "You actually — so this is you, from now on?" That is the thing with those pills — you think you're getting better, when to the rest of the world you are unbearable. It is best to take them in spurts, hurling yourself into a dry period until the world starts to make you sick again. She had been taking them every day for just about as long as I had known her. They flatten everything, making you feel empty and suspended, like a cipher in your own head. She had taken on a sallow, compressed translucence — her body no longer felt like a real thing so much as a wax model. How are you supposed to tell someone that her whole life is based on a stupid lie?

The construction site gave way to wide, empty streets lined with enormous steel and concrete structures that appeared to levitate in the night, suspended by unseen buttresses. Thin, crescent-shaped skyscrapers balanced on inverted concrete pyramids, as if forever on tiptoe. The sidewalks were canted to ward off the bums. Everything was skinned over in dark reflective glass, as if there weren't enough reminders around of how ugly we are. Something moved through the sky overhead, lit all over

with tiny red lights. I searched in my pockets for a loose cigarette.

.   .   .

I tried to get off the pills several times. I used to check myself into
clinics on a regular basis. First, the counselors strap you into a
steel apparatus, which rotates on two independent axes. It seems
like forever before they're done attaching the nodes. The head
doctor will look at some charts, take measurements, run your
blood through the purifier. "We're going to leave the room for a
while," they'll say, slipping into lead bibs. "Can I get you anything
before we begin?" The whole process takes hours, with cameras
all over the place sending invisible rays straight through you and
on into the other half of the world. Later they take you into a
room with pictures of your body covering the walls, millions of
small multicolored cross sections. You begin to understand how
comical the body is, how much a caricature of itself, how much
work the skin does in holding off this absurdity. Finally, they hand
you a vial of dummy pills. These are supposed to simulate the
effects of the real ones, but all they do is remind you of all the
good times you had before. Pretty soon, you're out in the night
again, shifting cautiously around unfamiliar neighborhoods.

.   .   .

I sensed that I was near Susan's house. People called this area the
Combat Zone. Each corner became increasingly familiar, from
the old days. Dark cars slowed up at intersections, their open
windows a provocation.

Her place was tall and white, set into a hill with a wide porch and endless spiraling stairs. Not much had changed since I had last been there, except for the cars in the driveway and the unnecessarily cocky addition of a highway yield sign next to the front door, as if to say to the authorities, "Come on, we dare you."

The doorbell didn't seem to be working. I saw the shape of someone moving through the frosted glass, and started banging. The form paused, turned either toward the door or away. "Hey," I called, "I'm looking for Susan. Do you happen to know . . . Does she —"

The form grew, swallowing the dim light emanating from a distant room. I stood back while a series of locks were undone. The man at the door was thin, dark skinned, wearing a loose white T-shirt and large blue jeans, thick hair barely visible beneath a green knit cap. A child, half white and half something else, clutched his leg from behind, peering out into the night at me with wide, dark eyes.

"What the — ?" he said, eyes barely open. Already, I felt stupid and alone.

"I'm looking for Susan. Is she still — ?"

Of course she wasn't there. Of course he didn't know what I was talking about. They never knew, one after the next. They never knew.

"Then why is all of that shit in there hers?"

"Hey, why don't you just —"

"I don't care what she told you to say. She has some things of mine. Would you —"

The man lifted his hands, palms out, pushing me out into the street in pantomime. "Go, go. Get out of —"

"She knows who I am. We used the same fucking tooth-brush so don't —" The man went behind the door for some-thing. The child followed his arm with her eyes, then looked back at me, something about the intensity of her stare turning me cold with anxiety. "What are you — ?" I said, moving back toward the steps. "Fuck is going on here?" The words came out of my mouth already rehearsed — I nearly choked with their hardness, the brittle, sharp shards of them lodged in me. He closed the door, and as I backed away down the steps I could see a hooked finger part the curtains of her bedroom window slightly.

The woman from the night before had told me I was uptight. I was like a sealed envelope, she said. I let her get away with it because it was true. You think that people only imagine they know you better than you know yourself. It makes you feel as though you're wearing your life on the outside of your body.

Across the street, catercorner, there was a restaurant that was open, improbably, at whatever hour it had come to be. I took a booth that looked out on the house, laying myself out on the cool orange vinyl bench seat, the most comfortable thing I had felt that night. A waitress came, setting the table with exagger-ated indifference. The fluorescent lights burned and flickered, turning everything a crisp yellow. Two old women sat at a booth across from me, staring blankly at each other, each clutching an identical ivory mug. They sat there, mute, in shapeless brown orthopedic shoes, some essential piece of them already dead, I was sure of it.

"Would you like some more time?"

"No, the coffee's —"

There were two clocks on the wall — one in Northern

Time and one in Korean, and only the Korean clock was working: 9:39, it said. I didn't particularly feel like doing the math.

.   .   .

Susan was one of those people who needed to be walked. If I didn't walk her, she would kick the sheets off the bed. "Okay, okay," I'd say each time, reaching for a bathrobe in the darkness, at the small end of an interminable night. The last time I saw her, the night after the census, she was feeling dizzy. "I can't sleep. I think I need to go somewhere," she said. "I think I need a doctor." She knelt on the bed, gripping the mattress, and vomited on the floor. I drove her to the hospital. We saw two police cars pulling into the emergency room entrance ahead of us. "You can just dump me off here. You don't have to . . . ," she said, hunched over in the back seat.

"No, I'll . . . You just rest." One of the cops got out to consult with the second squad car.

"No, really, I'll just get out and —"

"Are you sure?"

"Yes." She had her hand on the handle, her whole body rigid. What was I supposed to do?

.   .   .

The man opened Susan's door across the street. The three of them emerged, their heads snapping back and forth, scanning the block. Looking for me, I supposed. Susan held the child on her hip. Where had the child come from? I wondered, standing suddenly, startling the old women from their protracted, mutual reverie.

I made it out the door, stumbling, crashing into a pamphlet rack on my way across the street. Susan and whoever that man was ducked into an old wood-paneled station wagon. "Hey, Jesus —," I called out, picking up speed. The guy backed out into the road, nearly crashing right into me. Susan was busy in the backseat, strapping the kid into a special chair. Both of them looked at me with crazed, wide eyes, as if they had never seen me before. I knew immediately what had scared me earlier in the night when I'd backed away from the entrance to Susan's house — the kid's eyes, I could see right away, even in the darkness, were the same color as mine.

"What?" she said.

"You can't . . . you can't just . . ." Trembling, I was unable to spit out anything resembling a sentence.

"Get out of here."

"That . . . that? The last time we were together . . ."

It was hard to talk through the windshield. The man, her partner, shook a tight, vein-lined fist at me, cursing. Susan's eyes watered, and she bent forward in the way that I had received her, crying, on all of those long, dry nights. The scent of her hair came to me then, oddly. A tattoo on the inside of her arm of a flaming, sacred heart.

The car door opened and a foot came out. I bared my teeth at the man, taking a wide, fighting stance. We hovered there for a moment, trembling.

Susan covered her mouth, running her free hand through the child's hair. The child with her round, golden face — what features of mine had surfaced there, vying for some sort of attention? Having tried so hard for so long not to look at my own sloppy, asymmetrical head, I could barely tell.

"Oh . . . oh, forget about it. Just forget —" I backed away from the car. The man stood his ground until I made it to the sidewalk. They peeled out furiously as I slipped into the shadows cast by the high restaurant walls. First the sound of the car disappeared, and then the sight of it, its glowing red taillights dissolving at the other end of the long, empty avenue.

Sometime after dawn I ran into a man I'd broken a window for once, back before the Voiding Initiative, and he handed me a sandwich bag. "Happy Easter," he said, because it was April, after all, and each bright capsule contained within, when properly digested, gave me the distinct sensation of rising up out of my body and into the clouds, where I would shine like a sharp, vengeful sword, cutting a silver swath through the heavens.

Gantry sat behind the training facility, hidden from the burning tower exercise by a broad stand of tall yellow weeds, eating the pills his mother had prepared for him, orange pills that tasted like orange drink, the ones that stopped him from doing things like cursing in other languages or petting the faces of strangers. His classmates at the Ministry of Defense Summer Day Camp were suited up in flame-retardant coveralls, strafing the tower with pink chemical gel. "Closer! Get closer!" He could hear the instructor, Colonel Roger, shouting through a heavy cardboard cone. Gantry was pardoned from the more stressful, physically intense group challenges because of his chest, which had been all wrong for as long as he could remember. He didn't like to watch his peers at work, though. When he watched them, he thought too much about the terrible acts he'd like to perform on them in return for what they did to him on a daily basis, and when he thought about that, he was almost always overcome by dizzying, paralyzing guilt.

The camp was for children who were too smart and resourceful for their own schools, but also for slow children who were bused in from the craggy, burned-out cities in the distance. The idea was that the smart children would lead the slow ones out of the darkness of their ignorance, or at least prepare them for a brief stint in the military. Gantry was there against his will. His mother wanted him to learn to defend himself so that he might one day come home from school without a bandaged head or carrying an IV bag or being in a wheelchair.

He looked at his homework. The first question was "If I have forty acres of forest, how many search dogs will I need to find a fugitive?" He slid the sheet back into his yellow plastic portfolio and sighed deeply.

A bird approached his feet, looking at him sideways, its head a worrisome cloud of nervous activity. It was small and brown, a nutlike handful of a bird, and it was close, closer than any creature had ever come to Gantry, even when he had food in his open palm, even when he was down on all fours, panting, calling the creature by name.

"Chirk chirk?" the bird exclaimed, peering up with one empty, opalescent eye.

Gantry stared back at the bird with a startled, open expression, one that told anyone who might be looking that he was a boy prepared for nothing, a young man on whom any number of people could mount themselves, bury their heels in his soft, shapeless flanks, and thrust away at his life until all that was left was the shredded, musky rind.

"Spare a dime?" the bird asked in a voice that sounded thin and frail, born somewhere else in a flurry of spastic air.

"Beg pardon?" Gantry said.

"Got any change for a wayward sparrow?" the bird asked, retracting one of its slim, scaly legs into the downy mass of feathers covering its bright red breast.

"I don't have any money," said Gantry, pulling at his pockets to suggest their emptiness, "and anyway, you're full of crap. No sparrow's got red on it."

The bird's mouth opened again, wider this time. The lower beak slid back mechanically, and from the resulting hole a tiny human arm protruded, giving Gantry the finger. He looked up and saw Mr. Cushing and Mr. Felt off at the other end of the facility, past the obstacle course, holding a small remote, laughing and cursing. Mr. Cushing was the one who put a bag of fire in Gantry's locker. Mr. Felt was the one who had called Gantry "cum shovel" and drew the picture of two sheep doing it with a tree trunk on his forehead during Sleep Deprivation Workshop, which was where all of the slow kids were put when the instructors ran out of things for them to do. Gantry had seven Sleep Deprivation sessions today and gym and lunch, which was called a class only if you were slow and had to keep saying things like "this is an apple" while you ate the apple.

And now Gantry was hiding in the weeds, staring at the tiny, bare arm protruding from the bird's mouth, middle finger proudly erect in the breeze. He always hid in the weeds whenever he could, because that was the only place no one would follow him. Most people at camp followed him because they knew that sooner or later he was going to get worked over, and that was something they liked to see. He could not understand why he'd been singled out. There were uglier children, and slower ones — a few could barely even walk, and yet they were spared. There was no making sense of it. The beatings had gotten worse in the past few weeks. Gantry had to wear a face mask during Biochemical Trauma Reenactment, when the others would hurl things at him, one time even a burning oil drum, the impact of which made Gantry bleed from the ass a little. He hid this from everyone but his mom's friend Conrad. One night he shuffled into the family room with a clutch of toilet paper, in the center of which bloomed a bright red stain. Conrad, who'd lived in Gantry's house for nearly a year, hugged him and told him he was honored that Gantry had shared this private moment with him but did not actually mention whether or not such bleeding was indicative of a deeper, hidden wound.

Today the patch of weeds, too, was despoiled.

Gantry had four toys in his portfolio: one was a yellow block that was his mom; one was a brown block that stood for Conrad; a third, big red block that could be a car or a boat; and a small stick that could be a snake or a phone or his father, depending on whether he wanted to think about his father, a person he had never seen, primarily because Gantry was made when his mother's old girlfriend, Shelf, emptied the contents of an aluminum tub into his mother's womb. He had seen a picture of the two of them standing on either side of the device, grinning, holding champagne glasses. A piece of colored paper was taped to the front of the machine. It said "Daddy." The photograph was hidden behind a bit of torn fabric in his mother's jewelry chest. Gantry had found it the other night while looking for money. He brought it into the living room, where Conrad and his mother were watching a program on elephants. "What is this?" he said, holding the picture out at arm's length. His mother burst out crying and left the room. Conrad turned to punch one of the oversize throw pillows on the couch. He followed his mother into her bedroom.

"What is this?" he asked again. No other words were possible.

"Oh, you know what that is. How could you have just — what were you doing sneaking around?"

"Is this my father? Is this where I came from?"

"Gantry, you know where you came from. You know that

Shelf and I" — and here she stopped to collect a long breath — "Shelf and I wanted a child. This was the only way. How was I supposed to know what would happen afterward?"

"What did happen afterward?" Gantry asked, but his mother only fell on the bed, covering herself with the floral sheets.

Gantry went back to his room and looked at the picture. Shelf had been gone for years, without so much as a stray hair left behind. He could barely bring her name up without his mother collapsing. But he thought about Shelf often, more often than he thought about his father, who he imagined as a rail-thin man, brimming with ejaculate, vibrating solemnly in a small, dim room somewhere in a nearby city.

There were Mr. Cushing and Mr. Felt, holding the remote control at the other end of the park, cackling, and there was the bird with its mouth open, giving Gantry the finger. He thought about crushing the bird, about how easy it would be to stomp on its leering little head and grind it into the blacktop until it was just a smear of plasma and wires. But then he thought about what would happen to him next, how they would fill a baseball cap with dog mess and make him put it on, or stuff him up with pebbles, or mummify him with tape — all things they had done to him at one time or another. He'd liked the mummification, actually, until his mom and Conrad had to peel the tape off one piece at a time. It hurt so much that he was sure they were taking the top layer of skin right off his body. But afterward they said they were sorry and painted him with new skin and put brand-new sheets on his bed, and he felt so nice and warm again in the darkness that he forgot about the dreadful camp and Mr. Cushing and Mr. Felt altogether.

But it was hard to forget about Mr. Cushing and Mr. Felt for long. They had a way of always coming back at him; they had a sense for where he would be at any given time, and they would be there first, prepared with tools. Once, Gantry decided to play in a massive leaf pile Conrad had blown to the curb with a blower thing, and they had been, like, hiding inside the leaf pile all afternoon, just waiting to strap Gantry into a rubber nude suit, a white one even though Gantry was mixed. They made him walk up and down the street in the stifling suit, past Katrina Boda's house, twice, while they shouted things at him from behind through a megaphone. That episode had even made it into the local paper, with a large photo in which Gantry's privates were blocked out by one of the radar sticks the police used to calm down Mr. Cushing and Mr. Felt. Colonel Roger was wicked pissed and made all three of them work the hygiene stand for the rest of the week.

The bird drew the small arm back into its mouth. It cocked its head and looked at Gantry with its other eye. He kicked out his foot gingerly to test the bird's reaction. It dodged the foot, hopping backward, looking him up and down as it did so, taking a brief, humiliating survey of his body, as if to underscore that even it was capable of taking him down. In the distance Mr. Cushing gestured wildly with his elbows as he maneuvered the bird out of Gantry's path, while Mr. Felt jumped up and down, cupping his mouth with awkward, oversize hands.

The bird, now several feet away from Gantry, bent down to the ground until its beak nearly touched the pavement, and spread its wings. Two slender tubes emerged from underneath, and Gantry knew he was about to be strafed with behavior medicine — Mr. Felt had copied the keys to the camp's biochemical pantry, and daily he pilfered tiny vials of whatever he could get his hands on. Gantry drew his limbs in close to his body, hugging his long, spindly legs, both hands clasped over his mouth and nose in preparation. One thing he excelled in at the camp was the assumption of self-defense positions — no one could touch his Stop, Drop, and Roll, his Henderson Shroud, his Top Jimmy. He started to breathe slowly and deeply. Behavior medicine was supposed to sting a little. But there was a swooshing sound instead, a great rustling of leaves, and when he opened his eyes all Gantry saw was the swiftly retreating form of a colossal truancy robot, in whose chest cage Mr. Cushing and Mr. Felt sat cross-legged, fuming.

It was time to see the nurse. Or rather, it was time for the nurse to see Gantry, because it was she, after all, who came to him and did all the looking. Gantry just squatted over the machines and grimaced as warm jets of air were fired high into him, so high he swore they were massaging his heart.

"Nurse," Gantry said between clenched teeth, "what is it called when someone puts something on you so that you can't go near them anymore?"

"Like a preemptive hood?"

"No, not a garment or a magnet or anything. I mean like a document. Something that says that a person has to stay a certain distance away."

"Restraining order," the nurse said coolly, unfastening the nozzle from Gantry's chest catheter.

"Exactly. So, what, like, conditions would someone have to be under for a person to have one of those put on him?"

"Abuse of some kind, I imagine," she said. She had a deep, untraceable accent, and her black hair smelled like rich soil.

"Like if she had a partner who was beating the shit out of her?" Gantry asked.

"Who?"

"What?"

"Who?"

"Yeah, who what?"

"You said 'she.' 'She had a partner who was . . .' you know . . ."

"Oh," said Gantry, his face flushing bright red. He did not want the nurse to know that the person he had in mind was Shelf, that his mother had put a restraining order on Shelf when he was four. The term was incomprehensible to him at the time — it hovered over him, bearing down at all hours. "No, I just meant someone, anyone, who was being beat up in some way. That's the reason people get restraining orders, right? They would need a restraining order to keep other people away from them?"

The nurse held a clear tube filled with Gantry's vital juices up to the light and tapped it gently with her forefinger. There was something wrong with Gantry, but no one had yet figured out the specifics of the condition or the cause. "Seems to me," she said, "there's no way to keep a person away who feels it their right to stick around. It's like keeping a wasp in a jar. Either they'll find a way out, or they die."

He did not understand the example. He felt as if *he* were the wasp in the jar, crashing against the aluminum lid, choking on the sweet, dead air.

Gantry stood in the wide foyer of the restaurant, waiting for Conrad and his mom to get out of the bathroom. The walls and ceiling of the restaurant were padded with light quilted material, so that children who were floaters would not be hurt. At least Gantry was not a floater. His generation had been the last to receive the inoculations, before it was determined that the inoculations tended to flatten out the forehead, putting pressure on the frontal lobe of the brain. Gantry's forehead was broad, firm — it made him look angry even when he wasn't, which was most of the time. But people thought he was angry, and that was all the excuse they needed to avoid him at any cost.

He pressed his fist into the fluffy wall. It sank into the fabric, right down to the elbow. In the corner there was a candy machine, half full of bright, multicolored lozenges. Gantry ran his finger over the smudged glass surface, taking careful inventory of each candy, naked and pulverized, fused into grotesque clumps from disuse.

"Them candies have been in there a year," the hostess called out from behind a massive register. Gantry turned around, terribly embarrassed.

"Pardon?"

"Them candies. I think they put them candies in there, like, a year ago? Them same ones have been in there since I started working." The girl was not pretty, even through the most generous, high-minded lens, but the sight of her made something heavy move inside him. In her plain, quilted one-piece uniform she seemed to zero out the whole history of beauty, render it irrelevant.

"I'm still hungry, though," said Gantry. He could feel gobs of blood racing up through his neck to form in awkward splotches across his face.

"Have this," the girl said, coming toward him, her left palm outstretched. Resting there was a tiny brown cake.

"Boy, it's a small cake," Gantry said.

"Yes," said the girl. "It's a private cake."

"How much would a cake like that cost me?"

"Normally it costs a lot, but I am giving it to you for free on account of I just stole it from the display counter."

He looked. There was a single missing spot in the fanciful array of tiny cakes under the glass of the display case. "Won't you get in trouble for that?"

"I don't know. Usually we don't get in trouble, we just get yelled at. Or put in the cold room."

"Okay." Gantry took the cake from the girl, lightly and inadvertently brushing the surface of her palm with his fingertips as he did so. Her hand was white and chalky, ridged as if she'd been immersed in bathwater. He put the cake into his mouth. Its texture was rich, meaty — it made the saliva glands at the back of his mouth tingle and spark.

"This is a robust cake," he said.

"Yes."

"I go to camp during the day. To fight terrorists."

"If you come to the back room, I could take off your pants and do things to you," she said, but as she said this Conrad and Gantry's mother emerged from their respective rest rooms with alarming symmetry, and the girl disappeared.

The next day the instructors wore black masks and attacked the campers, throwing nets over them while shouting in a foreign language. They bound them with nylon cord to stout posts in the basement of the facility and hung a plastic medallion containing a sugar marble around their necks. If they got into a situation they could no longer control, the instructors advised them in halting English, they were to eat the sugar marble. This

meant suicide, and for the rest of the day the students who ate
their sugar marbles had to sit in the guidance counselor's office.

Gantry ate his marble as soon as it was issued to him.

"So, can you find things out about people with that com-
puter?" he asked the guidance counselor, Admiral Sedge, who
was navigating his way through a database in order to pull up
Gantry's record.

The admiral only huffed, moving his hand over the smeared,
hazy touch screen. He was nothing but a grainy, oversize pencil
of a man, slumped at the other end of the long desk.

"I need to find some stuff out," Gantry said to the admiral.

"Huh."

"I need to find out where my mom is."

"Your mother is at home, son." The admiral bit his lip, tapping repeatedly at the screen.

"No, this is my other mom. She went away a long time ago."

The admiral stopped tapping. He looked at Gantry. "The
hell do you want me to do about it?"

"Where is she?"

"Gantry. You know I can't give you that information."

"So that means you do have the information. Good, now
what would it take —"

"Gantry."

"I just want to get this straight. You have an address or something over there?"

"I have nothing, Gantry. I don't even have my own address
here."

"You couldn't, like, give me a hint? A street name?"

"Please don't do this." The admiral bent over, possibly
adjusting a shoe.

"I wouldn't be asking you about this unless it was really, profoundly important. Everything about the person I am is inside her head."

The admiral did not respond. He was bent completely in his chair, so that all Gantry could see over the desk was the rippled aperture of his pants opening out on the small of his back, cinched by a flimsy belt.

"Is there any way I could be allowed to have her street address, a speech bead number, something?"

"Gantry," the admiral said from beneath the desk, "this is not the first time we have been through something like this."

"Those other times, okay, I will admit I was a bit frivolous. I admit that I wasted your time with the petitions, the demonstrations."

"You faked your own death."

"I faked my death and if it were something I could take back, you know, I would be holding it here in my arms right now as I speak to you. But what I'm telling you is that this is an emergency. This is the kind of thing they'll be making a documentary of later, after the dust settles, after the bodies are recovered. The camera crew will want your perspective. Do you want to be a part of that documentary?"

"No."

"Great. So if I could get a phone number."

"I can give you a made-up phone number. Would that help?"

"Yes. Thanks. Also, I think Mr. Cushing is going to kill me when he gets out of jail again."

Shelf was not in the phone book. There were seven different entries for "Shelf," but none of them was the right Shelf. Gantry knew this because he called each one, asking, "Are you alone?"

before hanging up. It was late. Conrad and his mother were in her bedroom, talking softly and moving furniture. They were trying to make a child together. "The real way," Conrad had said once, and when Gantry's mother had given Conrad a shocked, hurt look he put his hand up over his mouth and never said anything about it again, but there it was, hanging in the air in their living room, casting out a rude, penetrating light.

He sat down on the living room couch, taking slow, contemplative bites from a withered stick of beef. On the television, two men were beating each other with clubs in slow motion. The thing to do, thought Gantry to himself, the only other option that he could drum up, was to ride around town on his three-wheeler, going up and down every street until he found her.

It was hot out. The sky was low and wide, scalding everything with furious white rays. Gantry sweat through his face mask. He yanked it off and stuffed it in his pants pocket, pedaling hard. The houses were aggressively identical. He would know her house when he saw it, though. It would resonate somehow — didn't elephants return to the place they were born in order to die? It would be something like that, Gantry thought. A knowledge beyond knowledge.

He turned onto the street with the restaurant. Maybe the girl was there — maybe she would give him another cake.

"You," she said from behind the counter. She was not as awful-looking as he'd remembered. Or maybe he'd just gotten used to the way she looked.

"Can I have another of those cakes?"

"No. I got in trouble the last time."

"Want to help me find someone?"

The place was packed, simmering with customers. She looked around, leaning over the counter to peer into the prep kitchen. Two short men were working with diced beef, hurriedly chucking handfuls into a chrome bowl. "Meet me out back," she whispered.

He parked his three-wheeler in the bushes and leaned on one of the high, green Dumpsters, constantly readjusting his pose for an imagined audience that he felt followed him everywhere, even into sleep. His dreams, he suspected, were always under intense scrutiny. The girl opened up the window to the prep kitchen and stuck out a bare leg. Her body was powerful, stocky. He thought about the naked pictures he had found in Conrad's toolbox, how for years he had known what intercourse looked like but not that there was any movement involved, so that his idea of sex involved nothing more than a sustained pose, held perhaps for hours. This image was so vivid in his head that what actually happened, when it had happened last summer with Katrina Boda out underneath the Trusty House of Flavor, was a crushing, humiliating disappointment.

The girl rushed up toward him.

"What can I call you?" Gantry asked. "Otherwise, I'm just calling you 'the girl.'"

"I keep forgetting my name," she said, looking down at her tag. "It's Elle."

"Like the letter?"

"Like the magazine."

"Anyway, I'm trying to find my mother. You could ride on back."

Elle walked over to the three-wheeler. She spread her hand out on the seat. Her face lost its shape. "I don't know. I don't like mothers."

"Why not?"

"They spend the first part of their lives trying to get something out of them, and then they spend the rest of their lives trying to get it back inside."

"Huh?"

"I just get sad when I see mothers. They're always coming into the restaurant. They look at me like I owe them something."

"This isn't the mother that had me. It was my other mother. She left a long time ago and my mother, the first mother, put a restraining order on her."

"Really? Why?"

"I don't know. That's part of what I want to know."

Elle lifted herself up onto the seat. "No thanks."

Gantry put his hands in his pockets. He gripped the soaked face mask there. It was like a large, cool raisin. "What do you want to do then?"

"Just see you with your clothes off."

They went to a quarry, where some cars had been abandoned. Gantry held the girl in his arms, tightly, as if she were something to be hauled across a vast expanse of empty road. His shirt was off, stuffed into the glove compartment of a broken station wagon. He looked into her eyes until all he could see was his own burly, misshapen face staring back at him in duplicate. "Kiss me someplace that I've never been kissed before," he said onto her face. She withdrew a little from Gantry to take an inventory of his soft, whitened torso, and then ran a finger cursorily across his chest. The skin there had a translucent quality. Her finger left a red trail of engorged blood vessels across the milky window of his flesh. Gingerly, she took his hand and raised it, upturned, to her lips, which she pressed softly against the smooth flesh of his wrist. The lips made a mark.

"That was nice," Gantry said.

She moved closer to him and cradled his neck in hers.

"Actually, though, I had some place specific in mind," he said into her ear.

The girl pulled back. "What?" she asked.

"Do you know where the perineum is?" he said.

She looked at his neck, at the fierce bobbing of his Adam's apple. It was almost as if she'd just lost some of the air that was keeping her puffed up, as if she were a parade float being put away for the season. But she knelt down anyway, and unbuckled Gantry's Velcro belt.

"Wait a second," Gantry said, clutching her wrist, because it did not feel right, the whole scenario, with Shelf out there, somewhere, slowly masticating the most pressing secrets about his life. "Tell me if you know. Why do people stay in places they know they're not supposed to? And how do they know when it's time to leave?"

The girl looked down. "Are you not supposed to be here? Say the truth. I can tell if you're lying and I'll beat you."

"I don't think I'm supposed to be here, but maybe that's just the part of me that knows I am supposed to be here playing a trick on the other, weaker part. Like you know how they say that one side of the brain is weaker than the other? Maybe that one side is more powerful than we think."

"What does your body say?"

Gantry was tired of the conversation. He fell over, and the girl knelt beside him, gently kissing his bare, heatstroked chest.

The houses, as he slowly passed them in the falling darkness, didn't offer the slightest indication of the whereabouts of Shelf.

Through the shuttered windows Gantry could see only flickering shadows. What else had he expected to see? A woman kneeling by the window, weeping softly into her hands, keeping a vigil for her son? The absurdity of it all hit him hard in the waist. He pedaled the three-wheeler laboriously, cursing at his own gullibility as he huffed the cool, brittle air. Shelf was far away, as far away as a person could get, and who was she, anyway? She'd been his mother for nearly half his life, but he could remember only the half after she was gone. All he knew about her came from muttered remarks his mom had made to Conrad when they were sure he was asleep. The restraining order — who was that meant to protect? His mom? Conrad? Him? Why had he stuffed himself with Shelf so fully, when he really had not the slightest idea what sort of a person she was? Gantry tried to bring up her face, but all he could muster was a postage-stamp-size portrait, muddied and damp — nothing more, really, than an outline. Meanwhile, he had just run from the girl at the quarry, whose slushy, threadbare presence bore down on him like a private storm cloud. He'd woken up in her arms — after he fell she'd dragged him into the backseat of an old mustard-colored cargo van, and had been stroking him, gently caressing the back of his neck. He pushed her away, fainting again in the process. He fainted a few more times on the way to the three-wheeler, busting open his knee and cutting his face on a rusty exhaust pipe, but each time he came to he saw her, standing in front of the sliding door, one foot propped up on the running board, elbow balanced on her knee, as if to suggest that this was the sort of rejection with which she'd already spent a short lifetime, that she exuded the sort of familiarity that made people comfortable enough with her to leave whenever the thought occurred to them, and knew it.

He couldn't shake the girl from his head — where was she on the food chain, one notch above him, or one below? He could not tell.

The houses started to look different — cheaper and newer, which meant that he'd made it all the way out to the suburbs. There was no easy way home from there, because they wouldn't let him carry the three-wheeler onto the bus, and the buses had probably shut down for the night anyway.

"Conrad?" he called from a pay phone outside a Trusty House of Flavor, one that was built in the shape of a gorilla.

There was static on the line, and the distant sound of furniture being built. "Yes, son?"

"Oh, Conrad, please don't call me that."

There was a pause. He heard his mother at the other end of the room, asking who was on the phone. "Where are you, buddy?"

"I am gone. I have no idea. I got myself lost, hugely lost." Gantry looked out onto the desolate array of chain stores that lined the interminable boulevard. Bathed in the static cadmium light of the streetlamps, emptied of patrons, they looked like the gaping mouths of young animals, eager to consider anything that might happen to fall within their purview. Steadying himself against the glass wall of the phone booth, he described the shape of the building to Conrad, gulping hot mouthfuls of air so that he would not start to sob.

After a brief, muffled silence, Conrad let out a thin, calculated sigh. "I will see what I can do for you, champ."

Mr. Cushing was out of jail by the end of the week. They kept Mr. Felt a week longer because of the laboratory's worth of chemicals they found in his locker. Without Mr. Felt standing next to him, Mr. Cushing seemed slightly out of focus, his face pixilated and vague. He could sense this, though, and it made him more irritable.

Gantry was in detention because no one could think of anywhere else to put him. He was putting his toys out on the desk when Mr. Cushing was brought into the detention bay by two armed Orange Jackets. In addition to the blocks and stick, his mother had given him a green marble. "You can pretend this is your little sister," she'd said, placing the glass sphere in his glistening palm.

The detention instructor was a substitute and, not knowing what might happen, put Mr. Cushing in the desk directly behind Gantry. Soon enough, Mr. Cushing stuck a pencil in Gantry's back.

"Why did you stab me?" Gantry said, trying to reach his arm out behind him to cover the wound.

"I didn't stab you."

"Why is your pencil totally covered with blood then?"

"Your dad is an anal meteorologist."

Gantry was not completely sure what that was, and anyway, the thought that his dad could actually be something, actually out there somewhere, and not just the contents of a test tube, as his mom kept telling him, was comforting, enough so that Gantry let Mr. Cushing plunge the pencil into his back again, right in the same spot, and wiggle it there. Gantry leaned into the sharp point, heaving himself up and back, bolstered by the quiet, unnamed hope that the pencil might poke right through the small kernel of his heart.

Rough hands came at me in the dark. One daughter slept, the other one sat up in bed and watched them lift me by the arms, quietly and efficiently, and carry me out of the shed. She sat motionless, mouth half open.

The air was fresh, and then stale again. I was in the hull of some boxy trailer. A woman with dim white skin sat next to me. She asked in Russian if she could bury her head in the crook of my arm. I said no but she burrowed there anyway, driving her massive forehead into my chest.

We drove for hours. Then the vehicle stopped, and we were ushered out into the blue night. They thanked us each for our participation in the world, but that, as in everything else, our time had run out. They began shoving us, one by one, into a deep pool. The woman next to me was motionless, like a tree stump. I was shaking so violently that I thought some vital part of me might snap right off. One of the soldiers, a pretty girl in a floppy canvas jumpsuit, approached the woman, whispered something into her ear, and rammed the butt of her rifle into the woman's back. The woman folded in half like a hunting knife and slipped, head-first, into the muck.

Then the girl came to me. She grasped my collar to steady me (I was tearing up now, stuttering, my lips cold and rubbery, cords of milky drool *running down my chin, spoiling my nightshirt) and brought my head up sideways to her mouth. Her breath was sharp and cool against my ear, like an icicle. "It helps to think of the first thing you can remember," she whispered, but what I heard was "think of the* worst *thing you can remember," so that when she punched my back with the gun I thought about the time I'd left the girls by the roadside. They were yelling at each other, and I could not make them stop. I pulled over and turned the car off. "You want me to leave you here, don't you?" I spat at them from the front seat. They sat straight up in their seats, looking down at their hands, both sets clenched into tight fists. "Get out," I said. They got out. I gunned the engine and ripped out onto the highway, driving away until they were nothing more than two misshapen specks in the rearview mirror. Then I turned around. When they got back in the car I told them that they would never forget what they'd just learned. Now, though, I am the stationary one, and they are moving swiftly away from me. I feel myself getting smaller, a rough smudge swiftly becoming engulfed by the horizon, slipping out of their perspective forever.*

My husband, before he disappeared, built a tall, sweeping tent of canvas in our backyard. He cut wide slits at regular intervals along the wall that act as gills, drawing gusts of cool air into the tent, puffing it up like a white lung. We rarely used the tent when he was around, but these days I find myself there on a daily basis, unable to remember exactly how I've ended up inside, kneeling, completely still on the braided burlap carpet. On a clear day, after a cloud migration, the only audible sound in the tent is the billowing of its own walls. It is the most peaceful space I have ever had the pleasure to enter, and I believe that my husband knew this even as he built it. He was a diminutive, excessively faulty man, given to fits of rage in which he'd stab himself in the chest to garner pity and affection. I cannot say that I ever loved him in the way that I'd imagined loving another person, but he built things well. Maybe all he was doing in building the tent was padding his chances of being remembered. He wanted to carve out a space in my consciousness so deep and intractable that I'd be forever unable to fill it back in with anything else. And he has.

I have tried my best to render a broad spectrum of experiences from the period outlined in this book. But the translation bunker is packed with samples none of us have yet been able to work with successfully. As you know, a great deal of the behavioral phenomena prevalent in the Super Flat Times has since been banned. Because of comprehensive infringement edicts issued in the first year after the Great Severance, the air pockets in which these thoughts and gestures are housed have been watermarked and are unbearable to touch, causing bleeding, skin ulcers, and cramps. Our hands have not yet developed the sort of calluses necessary to massage these patches accurately, and as a result we have not been able to get at the nucleus in which the memories are kept. As a result, the history presented here is somewhat skewed. Certain events we are sure we witnessed in those times have not shown up at all in the air pockets we've been able to manipulate — we can only conclude that this missing data resides in the protected air. We have not yet given up on these troubling passages, however. A group of children known as the Palm Family has volunteered to undergo an intensive twelve-year program to toughen their hands. Each day they train with buckets of hot sand, grains, steel sheets, and burlap, working their palms against the abrasive material until a sturdy mitt of dead skin can accumulate. Additionally, each of them has taken a pledge of delayed adolescence, as the development of adult hormones can have an adverse effect on the translation process. I have lectured at their facility, located on the outskirts of a remote sea-level village in the Northeastern Properties. They are brave children, some of them already in their twentieth year of life. During a tour of the grounds, I had the rare opportunity to assist in a training exercise by firing spiked aluminum spheres at them from a small cannon on the development courts. Watching the unbounded enthusiasm on their faces as they hurled themselves high into the air to catch the projectiles with both enormous hands, I forgot for a moment the great sacrifice they have made in order to bring the remaining prayers to light.

There are other problems as well. Some of the prayers I've come across have been too difficult to translate. Something about them sets my arms shuddering, makes my mouth go cold and sour. I've returned to the translation bunker many times, if only to see if I can build up a tolerance, but each time it's only gotten worse. The air inside the cabinet will fizz and shimmy even as I wheel it out onto the workshop floor on a steel gurney. I so much as dip my hand into the cabinet and black out instantly from the pain. I have a terrible, unstoppable feeling these are the prayers offered by friends, family members, people I have known for years who, one day, simply vanished. My mother, my father, Uncle Ramón, Soon Ok, Philippe, my two missing eggs — I am sure their final breath has been preserved somewhere in the vaults, sealed in a serialized container, indistinguishable in every other way from the others.

Should you take it upon yourself to continue this work, to finish translating the remaining samples before they disintegrate completely (and I hope that you will at least consider this), compiling them into a second volume, I ask that you start with these samples, which I have listed by serial number and ranked in order according to the severity of the pain I experience in coming near them. Should I live long enough to read your book, I would be curious to know what these people have to say for themselves:

7. Xddf-09994.5aff.GOLR-1_steft.cvr

6. Xddf-57433.9aff.CRFQ-8_chelm.cvr

5. Xddf-33R11.Daff.PPRF-6_broft.cvr

4. Xddf-00544.Xaff.MAZ-1_nger.cvr

3. Xddf-99199.4aff.LKII-2_jlurch.cvr

2. Xddf-88893.2aff.VROV-1_joliet.cvr

1. Xddf-56654.Aaff.VALO-x_xxe.cvr

Thank you in advance,

Mi Jin

Acknowledgments

The author wishes to thank the following people for their support: Cynthia Schmidt, Edan Cohen, Tom Lightfoot, Sandra Saari, Jason Bortz, Rachel Hall, David Kelly, Joanna Scott, Ken Cooper, Carole Maso, Gale Nelson, Robert Coover, Meredith Steinbach, Rosmarie and Keith Waldrop, C. D. Wright and Forrest Gander, Robert Arellano, Matthew Miele, R. J. Curtis, Judy Budnitz, Neal Pollack and Regina Allen, Michael Mezzo.

Special thanks to Ben Marcus and Heidi Julavits.

Special thanks to my family.